Style School

This Book belongs to

....

Kelly McKain

Date ....

USBORNE

My
totally secret
journal
by

Lucy Jessica Hartley

Style School Rules!

<u>Saturday the 11th of June,</u>
at after-lunch o'clock.
Sssssshhhhhhh!!!!!!
(I will tell you why I am
doing shushing in a minute!)

𝓗i girls! I am starting this new totally secret journal that I got at the Spend and Save 'cos I've got a really secret secret and I'm bursting to write about it!

The reason my really secret secret is really really secret is because if Mr. Cain (who is the School Uniform Police) finds out he will kill me into pulverized deadness. So whatever I write in between the covers of this journal is really really secretly secret and only between me and you, so that is why I am going sssssssshhhhhh!!!

Basically what happened is that recently I was in charge of doing the fashion pages for the school mag, with Simon Driscott. You are probably thinking, *Eh?* because as you know he is not a great choice of *Partner in Style* because of his lopsided haircut and weird hand signals out of *Star Trek* and complete failure to understand why he shouldn't do his tie in a kipper. But in fact what he lacked in *Fashion Sense* he made up for in *Having A Great Camera-ness* and *Technologicality Skills*. Also he had the good ability of listening to me and doing what I said with no arguing, so the fashion shoot all went really well.

Well, the point is that the mag came out just before half-term and everyone thought it was really cool. This girl Gemma from Year 7 kept coming up and asking me for fashion tips, saying, "What should I wear to my baby cousin's christening, because this yummy boy will be there?" and I was like, "Oh, that is a fashion emergency so I will most definitely help you." And just when I was thinking about an outfit she could put together I was struck with a flash of *Creative Inspiration*

(I have been getting a lot of those lately). The flash of *Creative Inspiration* was

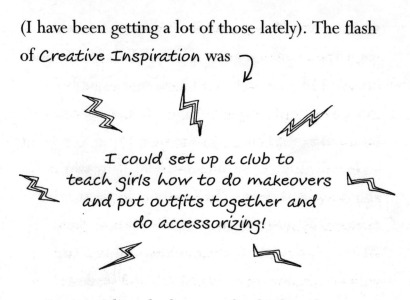

I could set up a club to teach girls how to do makeovers and put outfits together and do accessorizing!

So now I have had more of a think and come up with a cool name for the club, which is:

Style School

It will be *soooooo* fabulicious 'cos we can meet in the loos at lunchtimes, round the corner by the second row of toilets where not many

7

people normally go, and plus we can have field trips like we do for geography only less boring and no one will be forced to wear orange ~~cagools~~ ~~cagrels~~ ~~cagoolies~~ cagoules (got it!) and sketch industrial-aged bridges in the rain.

So anyway, I told Jules and Tilda (my two **BFF**) about *style school*. (**BFF** is short for Best Friends Forever, **BTW**.) (**BTW** is short for By The Way, **BTW**.) They think it is a cool idea and they are going to be my assistants for the first session. In fact they're coming over v. soon to help with the planning and that.

Then I needed to get some members, so I wrote this secret note and gave it to Gemma to pass on to any girls who might want to come. I have had to disguise my identity in case Mr. Cain finds out, 'cos if he did, well apart from him going completely nuts and his feet boiling in his Sergeant Major boots, something really awful might happen like I could get suspended or even *expeliated*. Oh, hang on, I think I mean *expelled*. I am getting mixed up with *expeliarmus* because Alex (my little bro) is right now reading Harry Potter, and he keeps springing out at me waving one of those giant pencils you buy on holiday that say "A Gift From Clovelly" and trying to turn me into things. He's got a Snoopy bath towel tied round his neck for a cape, but it's not very wizard-ish and also it is making his face go a bit red and bulgy, so maybe if I'm feeling nice later on I will run him up some proper robes on my fab sewing machine that Nan, oops I mean Delia, gave me. (She likes to be called Delia, 'cos being called Nan makes her feel old.)

If you absolutely *must* have a little brother, Alex is quite a good one, I suppose, except he is at that age where he thinks we should have everything absolutely completely the same or it's not fair, so he is often counting the chips on our plates and then getting me to give him two more or whatever to make it even. He tried to do it with baked beans last night but Mum said that

was a bridge too far (or a
bean too far, *hee hee!*).

Plus, he notices absolutely
everything and is always
going round measuring things
in an annoying way that gets me in trouble, like
going, "Mu-uu-um, Lucy has used two
centimetres of your Special Expensive Colour-
Lock Shampoo and I identified her fingermarks
in your Wrinkle De-crease Cream which you said
she is absolutely not allowed to use." Obviously I
have not got wrinkles yet but it is useful for
mixing with powder eyeshadow to get a smooth
glide-on paste.

Oh sorry, I have gone off the point. I do that
a lot, according to Mum and also according to
Jules and Tilda. Talking of Mum, I told her about
my *style school* inspiration today 'cos obviously
I will be taking loads of extra stuff into school for
it and she will be wondering why. She thinks it is
a fab idea – maybe 'cos she kind of assumed it is

an Official School Club like Extended Maths and Computer Club that they have at lunchtime, and not just something v. secret that I have made up. It's so unfair 'cos if Mr. Cain found out about *Style School* he would ban it straight away, but in other schools without a Mr. Cain it would be totally allowed. I decided that it's probably best to just let Mum think that it is totally allowed in our school too, at least at first. It's not lying exactly, just sort of not mentioning the whole facts.

Anyway, to go back to the main point, I'm sticking in a copy of the note I passed to Gemma when I was sitting behind her in Friday assembly. I spelled swapsies wrong in this first one so I had to write it again to give out, but here it is to show you. Well, not here *exactly* 'cos I have run out of space, but *P.T.O.*....

Want to know fashion secrets and get fab new tips for looking great?

Come to Style School, a new secret club, in the girls' loos (duh, obviously! Like we would try to hold anything in the stinky boys' ones!) at lunchtime on Monday the 13th at 12.30ish (but don't all come in a group or Mrs. Stepton will get suspicious and shoo you outside for your Fresh Air And Exercise and you will miss all the fab excitement and secretness!)

Love from ~~Lucy Jessi~~

Actually I can't write down my actual name in case Mr. Cain the School Uniform Police (and my arch-enemy) finds out who I am. But I will give you a clue, which is LBPP. ←

Say the password to get in, which is "Tankini" (if you don't know what this means then you definitely need to come!).

This message will self-destruct in five seconds.

Okay, no it won't, so please eat this message after reading. Erm, maybe not, 'cos I want you to pass it on to other girls who might want to come. But remember, it is Top Secret with a capital T and S. Bring fash mags, make-up and hair stuff, and ~~swopees~~ swapsies.

12

I'm in Year 8, and L is for Lucy and PP is for Picture Perfect, which is the fashion feature I did in the school mag. Cool code, huh?!

Oh hang on, that's the door. Well, not that the actual door is going, "Lucy, there's someone at me!" of course, but the door*bell*. Just wanted you to know we are totally ordinary and don't have a magic door, no matter how much Alex keeps trying to turn it into one with his giant Clovelly pencil.

Anyway, it is most likely Jules and Tilda ringing the bell 'cos they are coming to help me with the *Style School* stuff, so gotta go!

Sorry

for the interruptedness –
it is now 2 hours and
37 minutes later.

Jules and Tilda have just gone home so I can now
write that we've had loads of fab ideas for the first
Style School session. It's so nice of them to be
my assistants, especially when they're so busy with
their own stuff. Jules is in this Drama Showcase
thing on Friday night where you don't do a whole
play but some readings and different scenes and
stuff. It's to show the parents what's been going on
at drama club all term. She's doing the three
witches' speech from Macbeth (which is a play by
Shakespeare, that famous beardy writer from the
old days when they all wore tights, even the men!)
and she is Witch 1. The 3 witches (who are also
Liana Hawley and this girl from Year 9 whose
name I've forgotten) have booked the drama

14

studio to practise their lines on Wednesday after school. In return for Jules helping with *Style School* I am going to go along and be the prompter.

Tilda is really busy right now too 'cos she has a piano exam coming up, so she is practising like crazy at home and in the little rooms you get at school round the back of the music building that just have a piano in them and a clock and nothing else (well, and a piano stool, obviously!).

So after we had talked about the Drama Showcase and Tilda's exam, and once Jules had had a cheese sandwich (which she usually does when she comes round mine) we got straight down to business. We decided that for the first *Style School* session we are doing *What's Hot and What's Not*, like you see in mags where they show film stars in their latest designer dresses and write "Hit" or "Miss" over it. So we got Mum's latest copy of *Celeb* magazine and cut out some cool and uncool pictures and glued them

onto cardboard so they stood up
like actual people, but mini and
flat. Then we made some "Hit"
and "Miss" labels out of Post-its.

I also had the idea of making up a quiz for the
girls to do (if any come, fingers crossed they will!)
so they can work out their *Signature Style*.
What this basically means is the look that most
suits your personality and that you feel most
comfortable in, like for example, Jules's *Signature
Style* would be *Goth Rock Chick* and Tilda's
would be *Hippy Boho* or something like that.
But, I am only giving 3 choices in the quiz
(*Trendsetting Babe, City Chic* and *Boho
Princess*) otherwise it will go on for absolutely
ever. I'll get the girls to create an outfit in their
style, and then we'll show them how to do the hair
and make-up to go with it. And also, they can
adapt the styles to be really, really individual by
accessorizing and customizing, which we are going
to do about in later sessions.

Us three are going to model one look each for the girls, to give them some ideas to start off with, so we had to pull out all my clothes and scarves and belts and jewellery and get all my jackets out of the Hoover cupboard downstairs and then later we had to clear them all away again 'cos Mum got a bit annoyed about the mess. It was *soooooo* cool coming up with stuff, though, and we all looked totally different from normal!

We are going to do nail painting at *Style School* as well, if there's any time left, so I have to get all my varnishes together. I also have to find some old stuff I don't need any more for the swapsies. So I better stop writing in here and get going!

Ouch! I have now got hand ache from telling you so much!!!

Byeeeeee!!!!

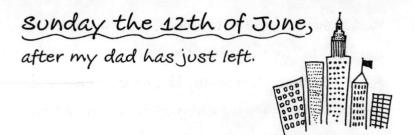

Sunday the 12th of June,
after my dad has just left.

As I have most probably mentioned before, Sunday in our house is family day, which means me and Jules and Tilda are not allowed to spend all day on the phone or constantly texting each other. Instead, Dad comes over from Uncle Ken's (where he now lives) for "a chat", which *actually* means scoffing all our Wagon Wheels, doing the crossword, and maybe asking to borrow the car.

It was quite cringe-making just now 'cos I made Dad and me a coffee (I am totally into drinking it now, and I don't even have to have four sugars any more, like I used to). Mum came down as well and we were talking about going to live in New York. Well, *I* was talking about it, and they were mainly staring at me in ASTONISHMENT.

Mum said moving to another country is *Not*

That simple. But I don't see why not when,

A) International flights are cheaper than ever, and
B) I can already do a quite good American accent.

I finished off by going, "We absolutely have to move to NYC, Mum, 'cos there are no nice boys in the whole of Dorset, or possibly even England."

Mum went, "Oh, is *that* why you keep going on about it? *Boys?* And there I was thinking it was to diversify your cultural experience!"

Mum and Dad both burst out laughing then, for some reason that I entirely did not get. But I didn't mind. It was just nice to see them happy together (well, not together in *that* way, 'cos they are separated, but you get what I mean).

I told Mum she'll be sorry about the New York thing when I'm completely old (like about 24 or something) and I've never had a proper boyfriend because of the *West of England Nice Boy*

shortage, and I end up having to marry Simon Driscott and becoming a *Geeky Minionette*.

"This boy obsession is very concerning, Lucy," Mum was saying. "I wasn't even *thinking* of boys at your age. Maybe I should check in *Raising Teenagers – The Most Rewarding Years* to see if they have any advice."

This informational book Mum is inseparatable from

Dad went, "Chill out, Sue, you don't need some stupid book to tell you what's what. I was really into girls at Lucy's age, man."

Mum put her hands on her hips and leaned back against the counter. "Firstly, I am not a *man*," she said icily, "secondly, I *am* chilled out and thirdly, the nearest you got to a girl at Lucy's age was watching your neighbour's sister sunbathe through a hole in the fence."

Mum winked at me and I did a giggly snorting thing of surprise and Dad got really embarrassed while desperately pretending not to be.

"Yeah, well, I was way too dedicated to my music to bother with all that," he mumbled.

I never in a gazillion years thought I'd feel grateful for Dad's music as it is so SCREECHINGLY AWFUL, but I am now 'cos it saved me from imagining him smooching girls!

Oh, yuck, I have just accidentally imagined that anyway!

URGH! Total gross out!

It's like, if I said to you, "Do NOT, whatever you do, think of a BLUE ELEPHANT," you would instantly think of one.

See?

So anyway, I suddenly wished that Alex's Harry Potter magic *was* real so I could transport myself far away to a land where *parents* never discuss *kissing,* or at least a land where I could magic 5 pairs of earmuffs onto my head to block out the cringe-making-ness.

Dad left then, with only *one* Wagon Wheel. He wanted two but I told him what Mum usually says to me and Alex, which is, "If you're still hungry after that, there is always *fruit.*" *Hee hee!*

When he'd gone, Mum did a big sigh and slumped at the kitchen table. "I don't know, Lu," she said. "Now your father's doing his radio show for students, he seems to be acting even more like one than usual. Maybe men reach a peak at say, 35, and then start going backwards, developmentally."

"That sounds quite likely," I went, "but at least you two are getting on better, with more laughing and less arguing."

"True," she said. "I just wish he'd be more of a *parent* to you. But then, maybe I should just 'chill out' as your father puts it and not worry so much. Maybe I'm being too overprotective."

I squeezed her tight and said, "Yes, you are WAY too overprotective. In fact, you should right now let me get my belly button pierced like everyone else in my class."

Mum gave me a bit of a tickle then. "I may be an anxious mum, Lu, but I wasn't born yesterday!" she snorted. "No one in your class has a belly button ring, henna hand tattoos, their own MAC make-up set or is allowed to wear patterny tights and high heels to school,

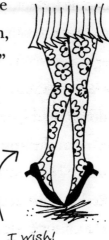

I wish!

before you mention all that again too! I am *marginally* in touch with what's going on, you know."

Sadly for me, my mum is *totally* in touch with what's going on, so I can't get away with that much. But, oh, I know, one of my *style school* sessions can be about changing your uniform to the absolute limits of what's allowable, and maybe if we inch the limits out more and more and more, one lipstick or rolled-up skirt at a time, then the day will eventually come when we *will* be wearing patterny tights with high heels to school! In fact, I could have a campaign to bring *style* to school like Jamie Oliver has brought *healthy dinners*.

I was just now closing my eyes and imagining me doing my campaign in assembly and everyone cheering and throwing their ties in the air! *Hmmm* – how *fabutastic* would that be?!

Right, time to stop dreaming and make up the quiz for *style school* – I have got some

ideas for the questions but I haven't written it all
down yet, and it's actually happening tomorrow —
how *cool* and also *scary*!!!

Monday, in the loos

4 minutes before

Style School officially

starts – eeekkk!!!

I am sitting in the end cubicle round the side
of the loos where no one normally goes and it is
now only 3 minutes before Style School officially
starts – yikes! I don't have my bag
in here, but luckily I have Alex's giant Clovelly
pencil (which I have borrowed to use as a pointer)
and some leftover literacy paper, so I can still
quickly scribble this.

   I am writing this as a way to calm down
because suddenly I am massively nervous with
just really hoping that Gemma passed the note
round and didn't totally forget and that some

actual girls come. The nervosity is so strong that my stomach is threatening to throw up the seven-vegetable pasta we had for lunch (it is normally burgers on Monday but the dinner ladies have been doing Jamie Oliver's healthy eating campaign - fine by me - veggies give you great skin!).

Jules and Tilda are right now in the next 2 cubicles laying out their signature style demonstration outfits on the closed loo seats for later. That way they'll be able to quickly get changed to model them for the girls.

If there are any girls coming that is!

Eeeekkkkk!!! I wish, wish, wish a gazillion wishes for this to be a success!

Oh, that is someone calling out "Tankini" - *Yay!* Gotta go!

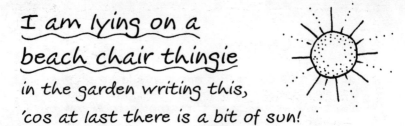

I am lying on a
beach chair thingie
in the garden writing this,
'cos at last there is a bit of sun!

They came!

Yessity-yes-yes!!

And it was really good!!! The girls loved it and
Jules and Tilda had fun in their roles as official
style school assistants.

I will show you exactly _who_ came by sticking
in their profiles (like you see on the _Hey Girls!_
readers' club pages), which I got them to fill in at
the end. I did the pix myself just now though 'cos
we ran out of time!

<u>Name:</u> Jemma

<u>Age:</u> 12

<u>Fave item of clothing:</u>

My slouchy off the shoulder striped black and white jumper

<u>Signature style:</u>

Trendsetting Babe

It is with a "J" apparently, how cool is that?! Shame I can't change the L in Lucy to anything more original!

<u>Name:</u> Lizzie

<u>Age:</u> 12 last Wednesday

<u>Fave item of clothing:</u>
gypsy skirt (I will love it even if it turns untrendy!)

<u>Signature style:</u>
Boho Princess

When we get onto hairstyles, I'm going to do Lizzie's hair in loose curls with Frizz-ease and then put cool coloured scarves in it!

All the girls are Year 7s, i.e. one year below me

Name: Carla

Age: 11

Fave item of clothing:

My skinny jeans

Signature Style:

Trendsetting Babe

short for Sunita

Name: Sunny

Age: 11

Fave item of clothing:
my new black
trousers with
the heart key
ring attached

Signature style:
City Chic

I kind of know Jemma 'cos of her asking me for fashion tips, but I hadn't spoken to the other girls before (though I'd seen them around, of course, and sat behind them in lower school assembly). So we did all the introducing ourselves and I said about how *Style School* has to be a completely secret club because if Mr. Cain finds out I will be in *massivo* trouble.

Then to make sure everyone would keep it really *secretly* secret we all said the secret oath, which I invented last night and wrote out big on some sugar paper left over from a "Make Your Own Incredible Hulk" kit of Alex's. My oath even uses proper oath-ish language, like:

> *I do solemnly swear that I will keep Style School a completely secret secret, most especially from Mr. Cain the School Uniform Police. I swear this on my fave item of clothing, and if I break this oath I promise to rend it asunder as punishment, plus wear my tie in a kipper for the rest of term to show my oath-breaking shame.*

Brainy Tilda came up with that bit when I rang her for ideas last night. She reckons it means tear it up.

So that was all really cool and then it was time to get on with *Sharing The Priceless Gift Of Knowledge* (as Mr. Wright always reckons he is doing with us in English).

The first thing we did was the quick *Style Savvy* test where Jules and Tilda held up the cut-out celebs from Mum's mag. I did pointing at them with the giant pencil and the girls had to say "Hit" if it was a *Good Style Choice* by the celeb and "Miss" if it was a *Fashion Disaster* and stick on the Post-its. They did really well actually and I loved being the teacher and I even tried out a teacher-ish phrase by going:

THAT CHAIR'S GOT FOUR LEGS – I SUGGEST YOU USE THEM ALL!

even though no one was actually sitting on a chair.

Oh dear, Mum has just come out here herself to read her *Celeb* mag for 10 minutes while the potatoes boil and has opened it to find loads of

empty spaces where the celebs should be.
Whoopsie!!! (I have promised to buy her a new
one tomorrow, if she can lend me the £1.70.)

Anyway, next we did the *Signature Style* quiz
that I made up to find out what kind of look suits
each girl's personality (I have stuck it at the back
of this journal in case you want to have a go too!).
When we had done the quiz and the girls had
worked out what style they were most like, me and
Jules and Tilda quickly ran into the loo cubicles,
which we had put signs on saying:

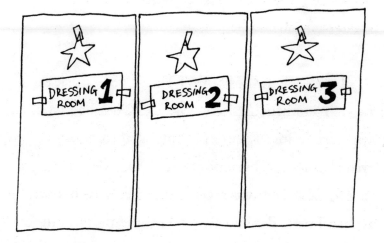

Then we came out in each of the different looks, like:

Trendsetting Babe   City Chic   Boho Princess

That's when these other Year 7 girls stuck their heads round the first row of loos and asked what we were doing. I suddenly panicked that they would tell a teacher about us. (I hadn't even *thought* about what to say to other girls coming in the loos!!) But luckily Carla came up with the cool idea of saying that we were checking our costumes for the Drama Showcase and Miss Rake said we could be in there. Isn't it amazing how when you say anything is for school people instantly stop being interested? It saved our onions anyway. (Oh, hang on, I think I mean our *bacon*!)

Other girls came into the loos, obviously, but they mostly stayed round the main side and didn't bother even looking at us. I suppose to the Year 10s and 11s we are too minutely young for them to even care about, 'cos they have way more important things to worry about like their exams and getting a boyfriend who has a car.

Then we had the *swap shop* and it was really fun, except Carla only had one glittery clip to swap and she really wanted my blue denim skirt that I have grown out of, so I let her have it for no swapsies, but just free. Jules got grumpy then 'cos she said I wouldn't even *lend* it to her and now I am giving it away, and Carla went all pale and scared of Jules, but I said, "Jules, that was one and a half years ago when it was brand new and there is no way it would fit you now anyway."

"Whatever. I'm just saying," Jules grumped, and I decided we should move on to our last activity so she would forget about the skirt and cheer up. So we did painting each other's nails and adding cool glitter nail tattoos that I got free off the cover of *Hey Girls!* (We will have to go round with our sleeves over our hands so Mr. Cain doesn't notice them!)

We all did our little fingernails the same colour (Purple Haze, brought in by Jemma) as a secret sign that we are in *Style School*. When we pass in the corridor and

stuff we are all going to waggle our *Purple Haze Pinkies* at each other as a sign to show we are in a secret club. Jules and Tilda had theirs done too, even though Tilda left her other fingers plain 'cos her dad is really stricty about nail varnish and Jules coloured her others in with black marker – NOT v. fashiony, but still.

While we were doing our nails I announced that there will be a *Style School* field trip on Wednesday after school to this cool shop called Beaujangles where we will be learning about accessories, which are a Girl's Best Friend.

I also said how they should each bring a normal pair of jeans and a plain T-shirt to wear for Reasons That Would Be Revealed Later.

I added, "But don't worry, this field trip will not involve orange cagoules," in case they were worried about that.

And I explained that for their *Style School* homework they had to design their own *Signature Style* outfit using the fash mags I lent them for inspiration (apart from Jemma 'cos she's already got a huge pile of her own) and using their new swapsies and stuff they've got at home. They have to bring the outfits to the next meeting, which is on Thursday, and then we'll design the make-up and hair to go with their look. How cool is that?!

Then we took everything down and packed it all away, so you would never actually know *style school* had happened.

When the bell went I got the girls to carefully slip back into the corridor one by one and blend in with the people coming in from break, so no one got suspicious. Tilda went first 'cos she hates being even one minute late. As they were leaving, Lizzie said how good *style school* was and Carla even asked for my autograph for being the Girlsworld model, which was just so cool and made me feel like an actual famous person.

Me and Jules modelled in a fashion shoot for the school mag and the pix ended up being used as advertising in the actual Girlsworld shop in town!

When all the girls had gone, I suddenly realized that Jules had not. And that's also when I realized that she was banging on the toilet wall going, "Help, help!"

So I had to quickly rescue her from where she was stuck inside the sleeve of the black polo neck

38

from demonstrating *City Chic-ness*. She was in a very *dark and stormy* mood, going, "That's not fair! I was the Girlsworld model too and Carla didn't ask for *my* autograph!"

"Well, she would've done if you weren't stuck in that top," I pointed out. But sadly that didn't make Jules any less fumy.

"And plus, Wednesday night is my rehearsal for the Drama Showcase," she grumped. "You promised to come. How could you go and stick a *Style School* field trip at the exact same time as I need you to be my prompter?"

I was thinking, *Oh no - quel désastre!* "I completely forgot," I told Jules. "Why didn't you remind me when I was saying it?"

"Hello? My head was trapped inside a sleeve in case you hadn't noticed," she went, all bolshily. She gave me a *Look of Poison* then, like it was all my fault she'd got stuck and hadn't been able to say anything. "Why can't you do it tomorrow night?" she asked.

"'Cos the Year 7s have netball practice after school," I told her.

"Oooohhh, the Year 7s! They're so important!" she went sarkily. "We have to make everything fit round them!"

I was going to say, *Well, duh, obviously, seeing as Style School is made out of Year 7s,* but when Jules is so massively moody the only thing you can really do is be ultra, ultra nice, so instead I went, "Oh, please let me off this once my lovely **BFF** and I promise I will always help you at every single drama rehearsal in the future for ever and ever! Oh, pleasy, please, please!"

Jules stayed a bit grumpy of course, but she did say I can do the field trip instead, so long as I give her a packet of Starbursts.

That is *soooooo* lucky – for a minute I thought that the *Style School* field trip was going to cause a big argument. But everything is fine, so **phew!!!**

<u>Tuesday night,</u>
lying on my bed eating the
Wagon Wheel that I saved
from Dad's clutches - *yum!!!*

$\mathcal{I}$ am just now about to make some notes for my talk on accessories that I am doing on our *style school* field trip tomorrow, but first I wanted to quickly write in here about something *totally fab* that got announced in assembly.

Just before the *totally fab* thing got announced, Mr. Phillips, the Head, was doing his speechy bit about the Good Samaritan, but trying to make it more hip for the kidz by rapping it, which was so completely embarrassing I wanted to curl up and die of *mortification*. But then assembly went from **CRINGE** to **COOL** 'cos he told us about the Charity Fayre we are having in the playground next Friday to raise money for the *Farms for Inner City Kids Fund*, which is our school charity.

41

I think the *Farms for Inner City Kids Fund* would work better as an exchange programme than a charity, 'cos I would love to go and live in an inner city like London, with all the hustle and bustle and fashion and music and excitement and 27 types of coffee you can get, instead of being constantly surrounded by the boringness of fields.

Anyway, Mr. Phillips explained that you can sign up for a stall and think of something to do on it to raise money, like a Hoopla or something. If your stall raises the most you could even win a little prize too, which is for *motivation*, although they are not revealing what it is yet. (Maybe 3 tickets to New York? How cool would that be?!) When the announcement was announced, I got instantly excited and started saying, "Let's go in for it," to Jules and Tilda, even though Mr. Phillips hadn't quite finished the assembly (*whoops!*), and Mr. Cain raised his whole single eyebrow at me to mean, *Be quiet, young lady.*

But then it was really funny 'cos Mr. Phillips

announced that it would be *Non-Uniform Day* next Friday as well, for 50p each, to make even more money for the farm charity. When he said that, Mr. Cain went really purple and his feet were probably boiling in his Sergeant Major boots, 'cos School Uniform is his *main passion* and making us wear it all correctly with no skirts rolled up or jumpers sloping off shoulders or accidental make-up on is his *main hobby*. When he sees us all dressed exactly how we want next Friday in our jeans and sparkly tops and that, with loads of nail polish and lippy and accessories, his brain will most probably go into overload. Then he will just *spontaneously combust*, which is an actual real thing that can happen where you just suddenly burst into flames for no reason.

While each row was filing out of the hall, we were all having a chat about ideas we might do for the Charity Fayre. The okay boys in my class like Ben Jones and Bill Cripps and Jamie Cousins are doing Beat The Goalie (well, of course it would be something to do with football!) and Augusta Rinaldi's lot are planning to use the CDT room to make one of those bendy wire things you have to weave a hoop round without making it buzz. I asked Simon Driscott what he was doing and he said really quietly in a whisper, "I cannot reveal that."

But I have to know stuff because of my *Natural Curiosity*, so I went, "Oh, pleasity-please-please tell me. I promise I won't tell a single living person. You can trust me 'cos of us being sort of friends with no fancying going on whatsoever."

Simon Driscott sighed and went, "Okay, but only because it's you. We're building a Virtual Reality machine and then we're going to charge 50p for each go in it."

Hmm, I was thinking, *so Simon Driscott is doing something computery – quel surprise, NOT!* "But won't that be a bit hard, even with your powers of *technologicality*?" I asked.

"We can handle it," he said, in a gravelishly serious voice like he was in charge of a *Top Secret Military Operation*. "We require maximum security while my technical team set to work on the programming, so no telling!"

"By technical team, are you talking about the Geeky Minions?" I went then.

"Yes," said Simon, ignoring me accidentally calling his friends the GMs to his actual face — **phew!!!** (I used to call SD the Prince of Pillockdom as well, but I have stopped now since I found out that he is a quite funny boy and okay.)

"Anyway, I don't know why anyone would want to go in a Virtual Reality machine when actual Real Reality is exciting enough as it is," I said, but SD just shrugged and looked *All Knowing*, which is a really annoying habit he has got.

But now I am here at home eating this Wagon Wheel and having time to think, I reckon a Virtual

Reality machine might be quite good, 'cos I could create a reality where I had big you-know-whats instead of being in the smallest bra size it is actually possible to *get*, and also where I had got my Q ages ago and there was a gorge boy on the horizon.

Q is our secret code word for period, BTW, 'cos P was too obvious!

The horizon

At break, me and Jules and Tilda signed up for a stall with Mrs. Stepton, who is our science teacher normally, but who is also in charge of the Charity Fayre. I couldn't think of a good thing to do right then, but she said, "Don't worry, I'll sign you up now and just come and see me when you've decided. You girls have such great ideas I know you'll think of something fabulous." So now we have to do an extra-specially brilliant stall to totally impress her, plus raise the most money and win the prize in case it is New York tickets.

All break we sat in the little doorway round the back of the art room and thought about what to do for the Charity Fayre, and me and Jules thought about it all lunch as well (Tilda had to practise for her piano exam on Thursday). Unfortunately, we couldn't come up with anything extra-specially brilliant, but only stuff like guessing the amount

47

of sweets in a jar, which is a bit
yawn-oramic. Jules wanted to
do a five-minute play for 20p per
person, but Tilda says no way is

she acting, especially not in front of people
she actually *knows.* I think planning the *Style
School* stuff must have used up all my *Creative
Inspiration* 'cos I had no good ideas whatsoever.
Anyway, we are going to have a sleepover on Friday
night and think about it properly, because then
Tilda's piano exam will be over and so will Jules's
Drama Showcase, so we can all work something out
together as a three with no other distractions
(hopefully my *Creative Inspiration* will be back
by then, too).

Oh, and talking of Tilda's piano exam, a big
problem has occurred. And it's all because last time
Tilda took one, she was so full of *nervosity* she
asked me and Jules to stand outside the exam room
door for support. She reckoned that even though
she couldn't *see* us from inside, she would know

we were there and that would make her feel more confident and be able to play better. Of course we didn't mind and Tilda did brilliantly and got a distinction, which is music language for an A++ and all was *fabbity fab fab*. But this time it's not 'cos her piano exam is on Thursday lunchtime, and she wants us to do the same thing again. When I said about the *Style School* meeting being at that time, she got really upset, going, "But you *have* to come! You *promised* you'd stand outside the door and help me get another distinction."

That's true – I did promise – but then, I didn't have the psychic powers of knowing it would clash with *Style School* or that *Style School* would even exist! "But we don't *really* help 'cos you can't even see us while you're playing," I went. "And anyway, Jules will go with you."

Tilda turned all panicky then, saying, "It has to be both of you! Just knowing you're there makes me feel like I can do it, and anyway a promise should be a promise." And she looked so trembly and upset that me and Jules had to put our arms round her, and I had to totally *promise again* to be there.

Gulp! I was thinking. *What am I going to do about Style School?* "I can always get the girls going on inventing cool new hairstyles and then slip out," I mumbled. "But it's a shame 'cos I thought you two would be at *my* thing, to support *me*."

"Well, we were, weren't we?" said Jules, all narkily. "We helped you get everything ready and we even went to the first one to be your assistants and stayed for the whole thing. But I didn't think you'd expect us to go to *all* of them. We've got our own lives, you know."

I was a bit like, *Woah, where did that come from?* and it made me realize that Jules is still grumpy 'cos I can't make it to her drama rehearsal tomorrow night, or maybe 'cos I gave Carla that denim skirt, or 'cos I got asked for my autograph for being the Girlsworld model and she didn't, or perhaps for ALL of those reasons. You can never be sure with Jules. But even if she was still in a mood about those things, I didn't think she'd be *so* snippy with me. I looked at Tilda, but she was conveniently busy rustling through her music sheets and pretending not to notice Jules having a

DARK AND STORMY MOOD.

I didn't say anything back to Jules 'cos there is really no point when she's in one of her moods (unless you actually *like* getting your head bitten off), but secretly I was really upset. I mean, I thought they *wanted* to be in *style school* and it was something we were all enjoying together. But they don't seem that bothered about it. Why don't they realize how important it is to me?

Of course I will go to Tilda's exam like I promised, but I kind of wish she'd let me off when she found out it clashed with *Style School*.

Right, I am going to stop worrying about Jules and Tilda and get on with my accessories talk for the field trip. Jules will have forgotten all about her grumpiness by tomorrow morning and we can have the cool sleepover on Friday and sort out our Charity Fayre stand and everything will be back to normal again.

Wednesday,
at 7.21 p.m.,
am full of excitability.

Well, I took the *style school* girls on the field trip into town and we all walked together in this big chatting jumble. It would have been better if my **BFF** were there, but Jules had her drama rehearsal thing and Tilda was doing piano practice. In a way I didn't really mind, actually, 'cos I know they have their own stuff to do, but I couldn't help feeling a *bit* CRUELLY ABANDONED.

Beaujangles doesn't have a changing room exactly 'cos the things are accessories and not actual clothes, so I got the girls to change into their normal jeans and plain T-shirts in the loos before we set off.

When we got to the shop, which is up this little alleyway by the Abbey, we all piled in with mega-excitement. Beaujangles is stuffed full of the

53

most fabulous hats and bracelets and charms and necklaces and earrings and belts and purses and scarves and rings and bags – and every single other accessory you could possibly think of or want, like even down to sparkly mobile holders (this is where I got Tilda's one for her birthday) and key rings and badges and that.

So I got the girls working in twos (Jemma with Sunny and Lizzie with Carla) and gave them this challenge:

> Make your partner's normal jeans and plain T-shirt into a look that you decide on by using 6 accessories of your choice. Then swap round and your partner will model for you.

"Marks will be awarded for creativity and for selection of individual items and how they are put together for the overall look," I told them. "You

54

have 20 minutes to complete both looks. **GO!**"

So the girls started discussing what to do and picking things up and putting them down and it was really fun and like being on one of those TV makeover shows. I was holding some totally fab vintagy-looking silvery earrings up to my ears to see if they did anything good to my eye colour (which is this weird grey), when I felt a *presence* behind me. (I am developing my *Female Intuition* by following the instructions in my Teen Witch Kit that Jules and Tilda gave me, and so I reckon that is why
I have started sensing presences.)

I turned around and saw this woman with fab dyed red hair and loads of chunky silver rings.

"What's going on?" she asked me, nodding towards the girls, who were doing a mad rampage through the shop.

"Erm, they're just browsing," I said.

"Looks more like they're wrecking my shop," she went.

I was *completely mortificated* with embarrassment then. In my *Style School* field trip excitement I had remembered about the normal jeans and plain T-shirt-wearing and the non-wearing of orange cagoules, but I had forgotten to ask the owner if it was okay to do our field trip in her actual shop! The girls had such big handfuls of stuff I knew there was no way I could pretend that we were going to buy it all, and I hadn't in actual fact realized that they were going to make such a mess of the displays and everything. So I decided to be honest and explain all about *Style School* and the field trip and how we would be buying some things if not everything.

The lady smiled – *phew!!!* "Well, provided that you clear up afterwards and put everything back, I suppose it's okay," she said. "And maybe if you pick the best effort then the winner can choose a little prize, so long as it's nothing too expensive."

I looked at her in total *astonishment* and

said about one million thank yous. I wished I'd done the challenge myself when she said about the prize, but I wouldn't have had a partner seeing as Jules and Tilda DESERTED me. Plus, I don't think organizers of things can really go in for them, can they? That's what it says in the tiny print on the cornflake packet competitions, anyway, which I sometimes read during breakfast when I have finished learning about the riboflavins and Vitamin, erm, F and all that on the side panel.

The lady introduced herself as Rosalie then – how totally cool is that name?! I introduced myself as Lucy Jessica Hartley *(duh, obviously!)* and we spent the next 16 and a half minutes chatting, which is how much time we had left before the challenge ended.

Then the girls were ready and they had all done totally fabbly.

This is what they created:

They had all done such a brill job that I couldn't possibly choose the best, so I asked Rosalie. She picked Jemma for being *startlingly original* and so Jemma got to choose something from the shop. She decided on the cool beads.

We had a huge clap for her and I told the girls how *fabulissimo* their outfits were, then we put all the accessories back except the ones that they were buying. I got a load of these jelly-ish wristbands for myself too, which Sunny used on her *City Chic* look, and some cool glittery slides.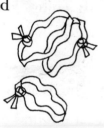

Then I was like, "Fab work, girls. *Style School* field trip dismissed. Don't forget your hair and make-up stuff for tomorrow."

My pupils all gave *me* a clap then, which I was totally not expecting and which was really cool.

After they'd gone I was still sort of hanging around in the shop looking at stuff when Jemma came back in and went, "Do you want to walk back with me, Lucy? We're going in the same direction."

So we walked really slowly up the hill, like at the speed of a snail on crutches (not that you can get crutches for snails, but you know what I mean). We were constantly chatting and we kept stopping to have a look in the cool shops like New Look and to have a laugh at the ones selling Tweedy Things For Old Ladies. It was so fab to chat to someone who's as mad on fashion as me. And Jemma's so stylish and confident and funny as well – she really made me laugh.

I have found out so many cool and fascinating things about her that I have made an actual list.

☆ *Cool and Fascinating Things* ☆
About Jemma

1. Her mum and dad have a flat in London as well as a house here, which is the most **FAB** idea I have **EVER** heard of. Maybe we could do

that instead of moving to New York! It would be good for charity too, 'cos when we are up there all the *Farms*  *for Inner City Kids* kids could come and stay in our house and enjoy the fields.

2. Next time they go to London for the weekend she is going to ask for me to come too, so we can go shopping in Selfridges and try on the really expensive designer stuff just for fun!

3. She has a sister called Chloe who is actually 18 and who has gone to uni but who drives home sometimes in her cool sports car and takes Jemma out to the shops and the cinema and pays for absolutely everything. Next time Chloe comes home Jemma's going to ask if I can come out with them too! How brilliant will that be?!

4. Jemma's mum and dad are working a lot in London and they also sometimes work at home (you do it by walking round the house with a mobile phone headset on, apparently). 'Cos they're busy she gets to do what she wants nearly **ALL** the  time. Like, for dinner she looks in this giant freezer they have got and picks something then sticks it in the microwave and it's like – PING! – your chosen dinner is ready and you never have to have anything you don't like (i.e. liver or strange veggies your mother is trying out like fennel and artichokes). Plus, she has no little brother counting her chips, even fabber!

When I got in Mum asked why I was a bit later than expected, and I said, "Because after the *style school* field trip I walked at the pace of a snail on crutches going uphill, but I had to 'cos that's how fast Jemma was going and, as you always say, walk with someone else if at all possible."

Mum sighed and went, "How did your field trip go?"

"Totally *fabulissimo*, thanks," I said, and told her all about it while she stirred this big pan on the stove that had a weird smell coming out of it, which is apparently butternut squash made into stew.

Another weird vegetable thing! →

"I wish *we* could have what we wanted out of the freezer every night in individual little portions," I said, when I'd finished talking about all the *Style School* stuff. "That would be so cool."

"It would until the salt and fat levels killed you," Mum muttered, serving out the weird orangey-coloured dinner, "and that's not to mention the expense."

"Oh, and I've been thinking that we should get a flat in London as well as this house," I said then, "so that we can go shopping in Selfridges any time we like."

I thought Mum would be ecstatic about my idea, seeing as how she loves shopping so much herself, but she just held the serving spoon in mid-air and stared at me. "Lucy, really, sometimes I wonder what planet you're on," she said. "Now, please wash your hands and call your brother."

SIGH!

I *know* what planet I'm on, which is Planet Lucy with embarrassing dads and weird vegetables and little brothers who won't stop measuring things. I wish I was on Planet Jemma with cool older sisters and flats in London and individually portionated dinners from the freezer. I know, I will cheer myself up by thinking of things for the Charity Fayre stall.

Still Wednesday,

at 9.55 p.m.,
under the covers in my bed
(finished my maths – yes!).

I am lying here too massively excited to sleep 'cos it is *Style School* tomorrow, and we're doing the hair and make-up and I have got loads of ideas for fab looks to try out on the girls.

I haven't had any ideas for the Charity Fayre stall yet, but hopefully some will come to me in my dreams.

Right, I have to go to sleep this actual second or I will look utterly horrible for tomorrow, which is not a good example to set my students.

Good night!

Thursday, first break,
on the stone steps by
the playground.

I am just quickly writing this for something to do 'cos I am all on my own – *boo and double boo*!

Jules has got a whole-group rehearsal for the Drama Showcase and Tilda is practising for her exam in one of the little practice rooms I told you about with the clocks in, so I can't even sit in there and quietly write this near her. I could hang round with the *style school* girls but they are indoors doing some kind of art thing for assembly.

Simon Driscott usually comes and talks to me when I have this sort of friend *vanishment*, but even *he* is too busy working on his Virtual Reality invention thingie.

Anyway, I want to write down about how things went a little bit wrong with Tilda on the way into school, but luckily it is sorted out now. Me and

66

Jules and Tilda walked in together this morning all linking arms (Tilda's dad dropped her round at mine) and I told them all about what happened on the *Style School* field trip and about walking home with Jemma and how she is so utterly cool and fascinating I had to make an actual *list* about her.

Jules seemed to be getting a bit grumpy, and then I knew she was definitely in a *dark and stormy* with me 'cos she changed places and linked arms with Tilda on the other side, when normally I *always* link with Jules, and Tilda goes on one end or the other.

Anyway, I realize now that I was maybe going on just a bit too much about *Style School* stuff 'cos even *Tilda* got annoyed and suddenly shouted, "Just stop!" and then looked all wobbly like she might start crying. I stood there gaping at her in FLABBERGASTED GOBSMACKEDNESS wondering what I had done and Jules gave me a *Look of Poison* while putting her arm

67

round Tilda to comfort her.

I felt utterly awful then, 'cos Tilda said all shakily, "I have been trying to talk about my piano exam for the last 15 minutes and you have been completely interrupting me and talking over me and not remotely listening and I'm so nervous and I don't think I'll even get through the set piece and, and…" Then she went all trembly and she had to clamp her lips together to keep from crying. I looked at Jules for help but she was busy going to Tilda, "Don't worry, you'll be fine, and we'll be there to support you, right outside the door."

So I said a **MASSIVO** sorry for going on about myself and then I did silly rhymes to cheer Tilda up, like going, "Tilda, I promise I will be at your piano exam,

Cross my heart, hope to die,
Ping my bra strap till I cry.

I have changed it from saying "stick a needle in my eye" as I can't even think of that bit without feeling sick – er, yuck, I just did!

Tilda said, "Promise more," but luckily she was smiling, so I went,

"Cross my heart, hope to go trembly, show my knickers in assembly!"

That one completely cracked us up and we were in helpless giggles all trying to think of another one when Mr. Cain spotted FUN occurring with his laser-like vision and came striding over to put a stop to it. He pointed to my big bulging carrier bag full of *Style School* stuff and said demandingly, "What is in there?"

I was about to say how that was my own private business and if he wanted to look inside he would have to come back with a *search warrant*, which is what people tend to say on TV detective shows. But then I decided that this is probably one of those times when it's better to just keep silencio. Luckily, Jules had a fab idea and went, "It's my costume for the Drama Showcase, sir. She's just carrying it for me."

Now that was a *Stroke of Genius* because if there's one thing that annoys Mr. Cain more than people having fun it is the Drama Showcase. It's part of his whole disapproving of personal self-expression thing, i.e. the same reason why he is so completely strict about uniform. I reckon his evil plan is that if we all *look* exactly the same like brainwashed clones we'll all start *thinking* exactly the same too, with no creativity whatsoever.

Mr. Cain did eye-rolling and tutting and a *Scathing Glance* towards the staff room, (obviously aimed through the wall at Mr. Wright, who is organizing the showcase) and went, "Yes, I understand that you have a rehearsal today...during maths time."

"Yes, sir," said Jules, and then we hurried away.

I was just thinking how Mr. Cain had completely believed me and was not suspicious of my extra bag at all when he called out, "I'll be watching you, Miss Hartley. I've got eyes in the back of my head."

So I got away with it, but only by the skin of my

Maybe he really has – that would explain a lot!

70

teeth, not that teeth have skin (what a gross idea!) but anyway, I will have to be extra-specially stealthy about *Style School* in future or Mr. Cain will be Onto Us his actual self and we will be Rumbled and also the Game will be Up.

Of course I straight away said thank you to Jules for her help and she went, "Well, that's what friends are for, to be there for each other and not go off with Year 7s, even ones who have flats in London. I hope you'll remember that, Lucy." Then she gave me a really eyeballing stare and flounced off inside and I couldn't catch up with her 'cos of my heavy bag.

Grrr! It is so annoying how Jules gets massively jealous of other girls being even remotely friends with me. I know she can't help it 'cos she's all Spanishly fiery and passionate, but there's nothing wrong with liking other people, is there? Especially when I can share my interests with them like she shares hers with the drama club people and Tilda shares hers with the other piano players and those brainy girls in Extended Maths. It's not like I'm going to go off and be **BFF** with the *style school* girls, is it?! Why can't Jules just get that?! I know, I will prove my loyalty to our three by arriving outside Tilda's piano exam before Jules does.

HA-HA-HAAAAAA!!!

Evil-genius laugh!

<u>Last break,</u>

sitting in the little doorway round the back of the art room waiting for Jules, but not for Tilda 'cos her brainy maths group find aquatic equations so exciting that they usually work right through break.

Weird how Jules hasn't turned up yet and it has been break for about 6 minutes already (we only get 15!). Jules is normally in my maths lesson (we are definitely *not* in the brainy group!) but she got off for that Drama Showcase rehearsal (lucky thing!).

Oh, I've just thought, we've got our normal drama lesson in the hall next, so maybe she's forgotten about meeting up 'cos she's stayed to help Miss Rake paint scenery or sew costumes or something. Jules is not normally a swot, but when it comes to drama she most definitely is because of wanting to be an actress. In fact, we have a deal that when she is a *fabulosa famosa* film star and I am a *Real Actual Fashion Designer* I am going to design her Red Carpet Gowns.

That doesn't mean dressing gowns made out of a bit of red carpet, BTW. Like this:

But more like the glitzy glam dresses that actresses wear for premieres. Like this:

I still have not been struck with any brilliant *Creative Inspirations* for the Charity Fayre stall, so I will tell you about the *Style School* meeting instead. Well, in actual fact it went brilliantly. When I spotted Lizzie in the corridor this morning we did the Purple Haze pinkie-waggling sign thingie, and then I told her to tell the girls to come to the loos one at a time, quietly, instead of in a gang all talking and that, which would be v. suspicious.

Jemma arrived first with a pink wheelie suitcase absolutely stuffed with make-up and hairstyling stuff and these twirly tongs you don't even need to plug in but that you just use with some styling gel, so we could even do hair curling! She is completely my ~~protejáy~~ ~~protegee~~ *protégée* (I think that's right!), which is like having a Mini-Me and really cool.

Before we started I made a *Security Announcement*, like you hear them do at airports, except this one was about Mr. Cain

75

getting suspicious about my extra bag and me being watched by the eyes in the back of his head. The girls looked a bit confused about that, so I just said, "Basically, be careful of Mr. Cain 'cos he could be *Onto Us*."

After that the girls went into the loo cubicles and got changed into the outfits they had put together to suit their personality types, based on the quiz we did last time. Jemma's was all neatly laid out in her suitcase and she did a sort of *snort of Derision* (like Simon Driscott does whenever I try to convince him that psychicness is real) when Carla dragged hers out of a plastic bag. Carla got annoyed and said that she'd made the clothes go crumply on purpose to be ultra-trendy, so there. I think the real truth is that she doesn't want Jemma to be my *protégée* but she wants to be it instead, so I said, "Well done for good creative thinking," to be encouraging.

Then we got all our hair and make-up stuff and accessories out (including the ones we'd bought at

Beaujangles) and invented these whole fab new looks to go with the clothes. I felt like a fashion designer organizing everyone and tweaking things and I have even decided to start saying *sweetie* and *darling* all the time, like *Real Actual Fashion Designers* constantly do.

So anyway, we did these cool hairstyles with Jemma's twirly tongs:

Suddenly Sunny went, "I know, let's make *Lucy* over too!" That was such a good idea I think she can be my *protégée* too. In fact, maybe they can all be it! Soon they were in a whirl of putting bits and pieces together with the things I brought in and thinking how to do my hair and make-up. I borrowed one of Jemma's tops (for the first time ever I am actually glad I am a *Late Developer*, as Mum and the assistants in Marks and Spencer's bra department call it, 'cos it means I can fit into a Year 7's top!). It was this cool pink sparkly one that she got in actual Selfridges in actual London!

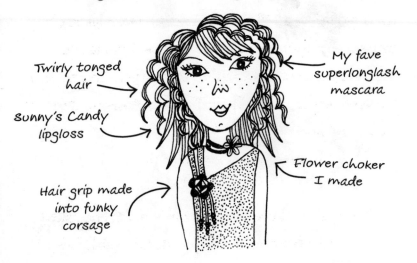

Twirly tonged hair →

← My fave superlonglash mascara

Sunny's Candy lipgloss →

Hair grip made into funky corsage →

← Flower choker I made

We pretended the long straight bit between the loo cubicles was a runway (runway is American for catwalk, BTW) and practised doing model-y walks up and down till suddenly it was only ten minutes to the bell. We had a big scramble to get changed and take all the make-up off (me and Jemma shared our cleansers with everyone) and put our hair in boring ponytails and that.

Mr. Cain's fun-detecting radar must have been on, 'cos when we filed out of the loos, he was standing right there and my stomach dropped into my shoes. He let the other girls go by but when I tried to, he went, "Just a moment, Miss Hartley," (for some reason he calls me that as if we are in Victorian times) and I had to stand there frozen to the spot wondering if he had totally *Busted Our Cover* or not.

something else you hear on detective shows

"Why have those girls got curly hair?" he asked me, waving a hand at the *Style School* girls, who were speedily scooting down the corridor out of danger.

Yeek! I was thinking. The curly hair was the one thing we couldn't undo!

Luckily, I had a *Creative Inspiration* and went, "They must have been eating their carrots, sir. That's the saying isn't it? It's probably these new healthy dinners we're getting." But then I remembered that *carrots* are for having good eyesight and it's *crusts* that are for curly hair and I clamped my mouth shut.

"What's going on, Miss Hartley?" he said slowly.

"Nothing, sir," I replied, quakily.

"Now why don't I believe that?" he asked.

"Maybe you're a naturally suspicious person," I suggested, but he just sighed and went, "It was a rhetorical question, Miss Hartley."

I'm not sure what that is, but I got the idea to zip my lips anyway.

"I know something's wrong but I just can't…" He stopped talking and peered hard at me and it felt like he could X-ray right through to my bones. "Aha!" he cried. "There's something odd about your make-up!"

I blinked at him innocently, going, "But I'm not wearing any, sir."

He waggled a finger at me. "That's what's odd. And your uniform's wrong too."

"But how, sir?" I asked.

"It's *exemplary*, that's how!" he barked. "It's usually *despicable*, yet now it is *exemplary*. Something *very* suspicious is going on here, Miss Hartley, and I intend to find out what."

Luckily, he let me go then, but GULP! I really hope he doesn't *find out what* or I am totally

DOOMED.

Oh, there's the bell and Jules and Tilda still haven't come round here. Never mind, I'll catch up with them in drama next.

At home,

snuggled up on the sofa
feeling TERRIBLE
(emotionality-wise, not that
I have the flu or anything)
after I walked here all by
myself on my own alone,
for an awful reason I
will tell you about now.

Oh *yurgh*, I feel *completely terrible* and also I
am such a *completely stupid idiot*!!!!

I am talking about **TILDA'S PIANO EXAM**!!!

The fact is that I *totally forgot* about it.

Yurgh! Yurgh! Yurgh!

As soon as I got to the drama room Tilda came
stomping up to me and went, "Where were you?"

"Where was I when?" I asked, and then I suddenly remembered. I had got so carried away with the *style school* girls making me over that I completely forgot to go and support Tilda, even though I had most sincerely and solemnly promised her I would.

I didn't even remember at last break when I was sitting in the little doorway round the back of the art room writing in here.

"I'm so sorry, Tilda," I began, but then Miss Rake clapped her hands to get us all quiet and was explaining what we were doing in today's lesson, which was to create a scene about conflict, so I couldn't say anything else.

I can show you exactly what happened next though (unfortunately!) because Miss Rake made us write it in our drama notebooks (and I am ripping it out to stick in here). She thought it was our scene about conflict when actually it was not drama but *Real Reality*.

This should be changed to
Destroying BFFness In Real Life

Exploring Conflict Through Drama

Our scene:

<u>Lucy:</u> Tilda, I'm so sorry. The truth is that I completely and utterly forgot about your piano exam.

<u>Tilda (upsetly):</u> But how could you? You knew how important it was to me!

<u>Lucy (apologizingly):</u> I got carried away with style school and the time slipped by and it just went totally out of my mind, but I am so, so, sooooooo sorry and I feel terribly awful about it and I promise it will never ever happen again.

(Tilda is about to forgive Lucy when Jules gets involved for no reason. She stands in front of Tilda with her arms folded and gives Lucy a most nasty look.)

84

<u>Jules (horribly):</u> I don't believe you forgot! I reckon you didn't come on purpose, 'cos you just wanted to carry on with your stupid Style School! And I also think you decided to LIE and say you forgot so Tilda would forgive you because she is so lovely. Well, I can see through your little plan, Lucy Jessica Hartley, and I think it sucks!

(Lucy is GOBSMACKEDLY FLABBERGASTED. Her jaw drops so much with the FLABBERGASTED GOBSMACKEDNESS she thinks it will actually fall off.)

<u>Lucy:</u> How DARE you say that when a. it is not true and 2. you are supposed to be my BFF!

<u>Jules:</u> Don't blame me! It's you who's completely forgotten about what BFFness even means! You should have been there for Tilda

85

but instead you were completely wrapped up in that stupid Style School. And even worse – you LIED about forgetting. Grrrr – fashion is so pointless!

Lucy: How can you say fashion is pointless! Have you gone insane?

Jules: Well, no, obviously I don't mean that, of course not! But it's all you ever talk about!

Lucy: No it's not! And anyway, you've got drama and Tilda's got piano and I support you two! Why can't you support me for a change?

Jules (yelling v. loudly): But we do! We helped with your Fantasy Fashion design, and with styling the boy band, and with planning the photo shoot for the school mag and we even came to the first Style School meeting to be your assistants! If you love the Year 7s so

How unfair is that?!

much, why don't you just go off with them?!

<u>Lucy</u>: I'm not going off with the Year 7s, but how am I supposed to have a Style School with no pupils?

<u>Jules</u>: Well, maybe you SHOULD go off with them, seeing as you don't care about us any more!

<u>Lucy</u>: Fine, I will!

<u>Jules</u>: Fine!

<u>Tilda</u>: Fine!

Very realistic dialogue and heartfelt emotion here Lucy, well done!

(A)

But of course none of us meant it like everything *was* fine, 'cos everything was in actual fact not fine at all. And of course I don't want to go off with the Year 7s, but Jules made me *soooooo* mad I just went *fine* without meaning it.

It was the first time I've got an A for drama, and I was not even acting. I think that is another case of *Irony*, which we have done about in English. When we all said "Fine!" we suddenly looked around and realized that everyone had stopped doing their scenes and they were all staring at ours (well, what they *thought* was ours!).

Suddenly, Miss Rake started clapping so hard her frizzy hair was bouncing up and down. Then everyone else started clapping too and instead of all storming out, like we were about to do, we had to do a bow and pretend it was made-up drama and not *Real Reality*.

Miss Rake started going on about how we'd really got the hang of "opening our locked boxes of feeling from our store of emotionality" or something like that. And then she said all the stuff I told you before about getting it all down in our drama notebooks which is why I have nearly the exact words of our tragic falling-out-ness to stick in here.

Then the bell went and that was the end of drama. But is it the end of me, Jules and Tilda as well??

How could Jules *be* that horrible? She acted liked I'd *meant* to hurt Tilda, by deliberately staying at *Style School* then lying about it. How totally unfair! I would **NEVER** do that!

We are supposed to be having the sleepover tomorrow to plan our stall for the Charity Fayre, so hopefully it will all *blow over*, like Mum always says it will when we fall out. But it would have to be a pretty strong wind to make things *blow over* after this. Like maybe a force 10 hurricane on that *Stripy-Sock-On-A-Pole Wind Scale* you do about in junior school geography.

But then, even that might not do it. Jules was full of furiosity, and Tilda was really upset. And I am both, plus **GOBSMACKED** and **FLABBERGASTED** that Jules could think I was lying to Tilda and also that one accidental thing has become such a massivo deal even though I have said loads of sorrys.

At school on Friday,

you will NEVER guess
where exactly I am sitting
writing this!

You would not believe it but I am right now
writing this from the computer room. I had to
come here 'cos there is no one to hang round with
except Simon Driscott. I have just been helping
him, but I am not allowed to any more. All I did
was pull out a wire that was really supposed to stay
in the computer, which made the screen go black.
But it made SD get really stressed for some reason.

I was like, "Oh, well, *sooooo* sorry that I
don't know everything about *technologicality*,"
and he was like, "You mean technology," and I was
like, "Whatever," and he was like, "Anyway, please
sit still and don't touch anything." So that is what I
am right now doing on this swively chair (and the
Geeky Minions are giving me *Looks of Poison*

for being in here at all which I am pretending not to notice).

Simon Driscott is even paler than usual from spending every single lunchtime in the computer room and if he and the GMs don't blow themselves up with this crazy Virtual Reality machine thingie they will probably all get some pasty *Lack of Vitamin D Disease* (which is the vitamin you get from sunshine, apparently).

Anyway, the reason I don't mind doing the sitting still and not touching anything is definitely not 'cos SD told me to, but instead 'cos I want to write in here and tell you what just happened.

When I got back from first break I found this note in my desk.

MEET ME AT THE START OF LUNCH BEHIND THE SCREEN IN THE OLD MUSIC ROOM. KNOCK THREE TIMES SO I KNOW IT'S YOU. DO NOT SHOW THIS NOTE TO ANYONE (ESPECIALLY JULES, WHO WOULD HAVE A DARK AND STORMY AT ME). LOVE FROM A. MYSTERY.

I had a strong feeling of psychicness that *A. Mystery* was in fact *T. Van der Zwan,* but I didn't do any winks at her or anything during English, just in case. Luckily, it was not Group Discussion but Individual Reading Comprehension, so we didn't have to talk to each other (Jules has still not talked to me since drama yesterday, not that I care!).

So anyway, I got to the old music room and did the three knocks then went in. There was Tilda, my most likely suspect for the note writer (so my psychicness is working – *yay!*) and I went, "No need for the spy stuff, Tilda. It's not life or death."

"It might be if Jules finds out I've talked to you!" she went, all dramatically.

I don't care what Jules thinks, not after she was so horrible to me for no reason, but I do care what Tilda thinks, so I went, "I'm so, so, *sooooooo* sorry again for yesterday, but I did honestly completely forget about your exam, whatever Jules

93

reckons. I would never ever in a gazillion years hurt your feelings on purpose."

"You honestly, honestly did forget?" asked Tilda.

"Honestly, honestly," I said, trying not to mind that she could even *half* believe Jules. Then I added, "Cross my heart, hope to go trembly, show my knickers in assembly!"

Luckily, Tilda still found that one funny and she did a little laugh and then we were friends again – *phew!*

"I just found out I got a distinction in my exam," she said, with a shy smile.

"Tilda, that's fab!" I cried, giving her a *massivo* hug. "See, you didn't need me there after all –" Tilda gave me an annoyed look and I quickly said, "But that's not the point, of course! Just very, very, very well done!"

"Thanks. Right, now you have to grovel like mad to Jules," she said, as if that was just a *Tiny Little Detail* and not a *Massive Big Deal*.

"You're not getting this, are you, Tilda?" I said,

calmly and sensibly. (Erm, okay, maybe more like hysterically and moodily.) "Me and Jules have been **BFF** since we were 5 when we won the sack race together 'cos of our co-operational skills. But now she thinks I'm a big fat liar, which is **NOT** true. *She* should be saying sorry to *me*!"

Tilda looked really upset then. "But Jules was only looking out for me," she cried. "I'm her **BFF** too, you know! Why can't you two just make up? After all, it's me you're fighting over and if I want you to then you should."

"It doesn't work like that," I told her.

"No, 'cos you're just as stubborn as each other," said Tilda, suddenly getting angry and marching off towards the door. When she got there she did a spinny turn and her plaits whipped round in a dangerous way and she shouted, "I was trying to fix everything before the sleepover tonight so we could be together as a three at the Charity Fayre, but if you don't make up with Jules she won't have you over."

"I'm not making the first move," I went, folding my arms in crossness. "I'm not the one calling her innocent friend a liar!"

Tilda looked at her shoes and shuffled a bit. "It's just that we can't all run the Charity Fayre stall with you two not speaking, and we really have to get on and think of something for it tonight," she mumbled. "And I did check with Mrs. Stepton but there aren't any more stalls left so we couldn't just have two separate ones and..." She trailed off then, going bright red.

I felt really sick realizing what Tilda was in actual fact saying. It was awful 'cos I really wanted to do the stall and raise money for the charity, but it is pretty obvious that Jules won't let me in on it, and unless I am going to turn up there and actually push her stuff off and put mine on (not that I've even had one idea for it yet, but anyway) there's no way I *can* do it. "Look, you two do it without me," I managed to croak. "I've got loads of *style school* stuff to organize anyway so I'm not that bothered."

"Okay, I suppose we'll have to then," Tilda muttered, and whirled out of the door with her plaits flying.

Of course I am **MASSIVELY** bothered, but what can I do?

Why doesn't Tilda get that it is not about her piano exam any more but about Jules being a really bad **BFF** to me? I know it was me who wanted us to be a three with Tilda, but I never, ever thought it would make Jules become her friend more than mine. And now I've lost Tilda too, 'cos of *her*.

I think it's another one of those *Irony* things that I have spent ages making sure Jules doesn't leave Tilda out and now *they* are leaving *me* out.

In fact, I bet Jules has been wanting to be a two with Tilda for ages and waiting for her chance to ditch me.

Or maybe I am just being over-imaginative.

Oh, I don't know! All I know is that the whole thing feels terrible and has ended up with me having to sit here with no **BFF**, watching the Geeky Minions typing stuff into a computer. Urgh, I've just had a V. V. **BAD THOUGHT:**

MAYBE THIS IS MY LIFE FROM NOW ON.

Grrr!! and *Arghhhh!!*

Friday night,
in my house, i.e.
NOT round Jules's.

The fact that it is Friday night and I am in my own house will tell you that me and poor Tilda and Miss Horrible Jules have still not made up. She will have to **MASSIVELY** apologize to me before I even **THINK** about making up with her, and according to Tilda she is not going to, so that is that. I kept thinking my phone would beep with a text from her saying sorry and inviting me to the sleepover after all.

But nothing has happened.

So I am not at the sleepover at Jules's house and I am not doing the stall at the Charity Fayre with them. I am trying to feel better about being left out of tonight by imagining them doing things that are only fun with more than two people, like for example playing Twister or Cluedo or Piggy In

99

The Middle or Wink Murder. But it's not working actually and I still feel totally miz.

Apparently, tomorrow Alex is having some individual *Father and Son* time with Dad to do *Male Bonding* and that, which Mum read about in her new book, *How To Divorce Without Messing Up Your Kids* (not that they *are* getting divorced 'cos they are only separated, but anyway). That leaves Mum free to take me into town, so at least I won't have a completely boring weekend stuck here on my own with Alex trying to magically turn me into things.

I haven't told Mum why I'm not really going to Jules's house tonight, but instead I said I've got a stomach ache. So that's why I'm huddled up in a blanket on the sofa with her fussing over me bringing me hot chocolate and feeling my forehead and everything (she doesn't realize it's the blanket that is actually making me hot!).

Yikes! Mum just came in and said if I'm still feeling bad tomorrow maybe we shouldn't go into

town. Oh no – I will have to start feeling better –
and fast! Only not too fast or it will be suspicious.
I hate doing *Fake Illness* and I wish I could tell
Mum the truth, but I just can't because she would
say we're all being silly and ring Isabella (Jules's
mum) and probably make me go round there
anyway, which I am *soooooo* not doing!

Oh, she's come in again now. Got to stop
writing this so I can watch TV with her and do
my *Gradual Convincing Recovery*.

Saturday,
good and bad.

$\mathcal{M}$e and Mum had a really good time in town and for a while I actually forgot about the J and T problem, which has been going round and round in my head all last night and this morning.

We got our hair done, and maybe Mum is in fact finally realizing that I am almost nearly grown up because she let me have a few streaks of these cool honey-coloured highlights in my hair. She was having hers done in the colour it is naturally, which sounds a bit like wasting money, but is in fact for *Banishing Those Tell-Tale Greys* as Phil the stylist called it.

It was really good fun, 'cos while our hair was in the foil stuff they brought out tea and coffee for us that was free and there were all these cool mags to read, although Mum said I was too young for *Cosmo* and she'd have that one, Thank You Very Much.

After that we had our hair washed again and cut and blow-dried all fabbly with curling brushes so it sticks out from your head in an actual style, instead of just hanging downwards like usual.

But then disaster struck. We were just coming out of the hair salon looking all fabbity-fab-fab when we walked almost smack-bang into Jules and Tilda. Tilda went bright red and started shuffling embarrassedly, while Jules looked really *dark and stormily* at me and I did that eye-boggling *What You Staring At?* thing back at her. Meanwhile,

Mum was like, "Oh, hello, girls, how lovely to see you. Lucy's feeling much better now, such a shame she missed the sleepover last night but still, couldn't be helped. I hope you had a nice time and I hope you had a good idea for the Charity Fayre, it all sounds wonderful and I'm so proud of you girls for making a contribution, etc. etc. etc."

she didn't actually say etc. etc. etc., but you get what I mean

"Yes, Mrs. Hartley," went Tilda really mumblingly.

"Lovely to see you, Sue," said Jules, "but we've, erm, got to hurry, I'm afraid. We've got to, erm…"

And without saying one single thing to me, Jules pulled Tilda along the pavement away from us and I thought Tilda would do a quick wink at me or something to show that we are secretly still friends, but she didn't. I think that was what they call the *Final Straw*, 'cos when Mum looked at me and said, "How odd! You girls haven't fallen out, have you?" I already had tears running down my face and I couldn't talk so I just had to do miserable sniffling and nodding.

Because my mum is so nice she straight away steered me into the Cool Cats café and sat me down in a booth where no one can look at you, and handed me a bunch of napkins out of the dispenser and then she went up to the counter and came back with hot chocolates for us and said, "Tell me all about it, Lu."

So I did tell her all about how I forgot to go and support Tilda at her exam and how Jules didn't believe me and said that I was lying and that I didn't really forget but just wanted to stay at *Style School* instead and I also said how that was completely unfair and untrue, and explained how I said sorry to Tilda loads of times and how *she* believes I forgot and how she forgave me but also how she won't officially be my friend again till

I make up with Jules which I am not doing 'cos I'm right and she's wrong so why should I?

Mum took my hand across the table and went, "Breathe, sweetheart." When I had calmed down a bit she also went, "You might not want to hear this, but in my opinion, you and Jules are both kind of right and kind of wrong here," she said gently.

I snatched my hand away then, and I was just staring at her with my eyes popping out. "What – you don't believe me either?" I cried. "My own mother! Char-MING!"

Mum sighed. "I'm not saying you lied, love," she said. "It's just, well, put it this way, if Stella Boyd had rung you up and you'd arranged to go shopping together, would you have forgotten?"

"No way!" I went. "I wouldn't miss that for the world! She could help me pick out some summer outfits, 'cos I'm never sure if those little sundresses suit me, and maybe we could go to Claire's and choose necklaces and maybe she'd even…"

I stopped talking then 'cos Mum was giving me

one of her *Meaningful Looks* and I couldn't work
out why.

"Anyway," I said, "why are you changing the
subject onto Stella Boyd when we were talking
about Tilda's piano... Oh." Suddenly I
understood. And then I felt very awful and about
as big as this:

"You mean, I didn't really try that hard to
remember," I croaked.

Mum nodded. "It's easy to get so wrapped up
in our own things that we sometimes forget to be
there for our friends," she said.

"And after missing Jules's Drama Showcase
rehearsal when I promised to help her out too..."

Mum peered at me, questioningly.

"I forgot about that as well," I admitted. "I
suppose I can see why Jules might have thought

I didn't care about them. Oh, I'm such a horrible person!"

Weirdly, Mum laughed. "I wouldn't put it like that!" she said. "A drama queen, maybe! But not horrible. You just need to balance things better, and make sure your friends know how much you value them."

"But Jules said some really nasty things –" I began, sulkingly.

"But Tilda forgave you," said Mum quickly. "Maybe it's time to follow her example and forgive Jules."

"Maybe," I said.

Mum smiled and squeezed my hand, going, "I'm sure you'll do the right thing."

So I have cheered up a lot since the café happening, and this afternoon has been okay, 'cos I have mainly been helping with the housework for my pocket money (including dusting all the mirrors and the TV extra carefully while admiring my cool new hair). I do want to do the right thing – I'm not sure what the right thing *is*, though, 'cos if I say sorry to Jules she'll think I really *did* lie, so I am still puzzling that out in my head.

Oh, gotta go, Mum is calling me downstairs. We're having takeaway and DVDs tonight, so if I don't go with them and choose what I want Mum will only take Alex and then we'll end up watching *The Incredible Hulk* (again!) while eating a pineapple and sweetcorn pizza – blurgh!

<u>Sunday, after tea,</u>
and after my
Father and Daughter
time with Dad.

Well, this morning my brain played a horrible trick
on me, 'cos I woke up feeling all excited about
doing the Charity Fayre stall next week with Jules
and Tilda, and then I suddenly remembered that
I'm not involved any more. I had to stare at my
new highlights in the mirror for at least 6 minutes
before I began to feel even one bit better.

I still have to work out how to say sorry to
Jules for forgetting and make her believe I wasn't
lying – without making her think I'm admitting
it's all my fault, when it's at least 45% hers. Or
maybe 44%.

Today I've been having my *Father and
Daughter* time, while Mum took Alex round to
play with Matthew. I wanted Dad to come round

here 'cos it was nice and sunny so we could go out in the garden – which you can't at Uncle Ken's 'cos it is a flat on the fourth floor without even a window box, plus it smells of curry and feet and has a toilet that, according to Mum, has *never set eyes on a loo brush*, so it's not that nice to go there even on rainy days.

When Dad got here I was sunbathing (with about Factor 1 Zillion Suncream on, of course, 'cos Mum insists) and sketching some new sundress designs with mags spread all

round me for inspiration. At first we had an awkward bit where we realized we hadn't thought about what we'd actually *do* together. I went, "You can go and put the telly on if you like and I'll stay out here," but Dad went, "No, I'll do what you're doing, that'll be fine," and so he got the other sun chair out of the shed and picked up one of my mags and reclined himself. I started laughing and he was going, "What? *Hey Girls!* is my fave mag!" in an impression of me, and then we were both laughing and it was okay after that.

Dad said, "I hope this new scheme of your mum's about you and Alex having individual time with me isn't messing up your plans for the weekend?" and so I ended up telling him how I didn't *have* any plans for the weekend 'cos of what happened with Jules and Tilda. Amazingly, he actually listened to the whole entire thing without doing what he usually does when I am telling him the *Vital Facts* of my life, like picking up his guitar and strumming it, or flicking on Ceefax to look at the football scores. And I told him how Mum said she knew I would do the right thing, but that I was still trying to work out *how* exactly.

"I'm sure you'll sort it out," he said. "And it was very wise of your mum to say that."

Then I asked what was up with him and he told me how his DJ job's going well (his radio show is 10 p.m. till 2 a.m. so I don't normally get to listen to it, but I did help come up with ideas for it when he started). He was like, "The listeners

sometimes come to the station to meet me and ask for autographs. Can you believe it, they actually think I'm cool? *Me!*"

That really *amazed* me. "But you've always thought you were cool," I went.

Dad said, "No, just desperately trying to be and failing, more like! I mean, leather trousers with big bunchy boxer shorts sticking out of the top, come on, who was I kidding?!"

"But you must have been cool once, being in that band and everything," I said confusedly.

"Nope," went Dad. "Your mum was right. The nearest I got to a girl at your age **WAS** looking through the neighbours' fence! And don't tell her but the nearest I got to being in a band was playing the triangle in the school orchestra. I just made that up to impress her. I couldn't believe it when she said yes to going out with me, she was way out of my league."

"Still is," I said jokingly. Dad was saying nice things about Mum at last, so I should have been pleased. But I wasn't that keen on hearing about them being young and going out together, 'cos:

A) it is weird to think of them as just normal people instead of as Mum and Dad and

B) it makes me upset to think of them happy together, 'cos it reminds me that they are now NOT happy together and have got separated and it doesn't seem fair that the happiness couldn't just carry on, even just for the sake of me and Alex.

So I did Moving Swiftly On, which is what you do when you don't want to talk about a subject, and got us some choc ices out of the freezer and made Dad put some sun lotion on his gross-o-matic hairy, pasty white legs so they didn't become revolting hairy, peeling, burned legs, and then I did the quizzes out of my mags on him, which was quite funny 'cos no way is Dad "a lively sassy girl who says what she feels" or even a "mega-flirt who needs to start putting her mates before boys".

Our *Individual Time* was so much fun in the end that when Mum and Alex got back I couldn't believe it was actually 5 o'clock already. Mum was really pleased when I told her later that I quite like this new *Father and Daughter* thingie. I also "accidentally" let slip how he said she was very wise. She smiled and said, "I take back what I said before. It seems like he's being a pretty good parent to you after all."

"Not as good as you, lovely mummy," I went, giving her a big hug, while noticing the fairy cakes she'd brought in from Matthew's mum.

"Creep!" laughed Mum, swatting me away. "And yes, you *may* have a cake, before you ask!"

So now I am upstairs feeling pretty okay about things, 'cos I have had a nice time with Dad and also a yummy cake and I have the *Style School* stuff to plan for tomorrow, which is really fun. We are going to take the outfits we put together in the girls' own style and adapt them into sophisticated evening looks by doing different make-up and hair and adding glam accessories. I've even put something together for myself, 'cos it was *soooooo* much fun joining in with the girls last time.

Day   Evening

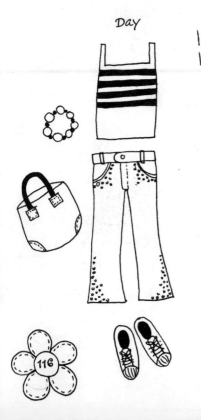
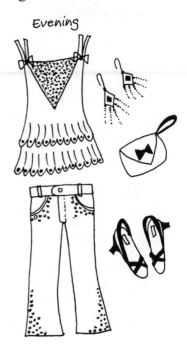

Cool, huh?

I'm thinking if we have time we might even make some fab sparkly necklaces from this beading kit Nan (whoops, I mean Delia) got me as well. You can wear them in lots of different ways like:

1) 2)

3) 4)

5)

That way we would all have a bit of evening sparkle that is the same, and it will be another secret thing to show that we're in *Style School*, like if we all wear them at the next school disco or a birthday party or something.

But, right now, I'd better go and get all the bits and pieces together for *Style School*. I wish I could ring Jules and Tilda and tell them all my excitement, but I can't. I really *really* hope I can find a way for us to make up. And soon!

Monday after lunch,

I am meant to be
in science, but instead
I am in the loos. Alone.

Oh, I can hardly bear to tell you what's just happened – it's too utterly awful.

I am sitting here on my own alone, on the floor of the loos not knowing what to do with myself. The bell has gone but there is no way I can go to science when I am still crying quite a lot.

Everything is spoiled and ruined and completely wrecked.

I know I will have to start telling you what happened, but it is so hard to make my hand write it. I wish it could just be wiped out of my brain forever and then I wouldn't have to remember the terrible things that Mr. Cain said, or my complete *humiliatedness* in front of the whole school, or the fact that I have got a detention tomorrow so

Mum will most likely go mad and ban me from fashion-related activities forever.

Okay, deep breathing, wiping eyes, blowing nose – now I will say it. What happened was the *style school* meeting had started and we were all in our home clothes in our different styles and we were doing the evening make-up and accessorizing and it was all really brill and fun until…

…suddenly the fire alarm went.

Well, we all completely froze to the spot. We didn't know if it was a real fire or just a drill, but we did know one thing, i.e. no way could we go outside like this – 'cos everyone would find out about *style school* and we would get completely killed by Mr. Cain (turns out we did anyway, but still).

So the fire bell was going *brrrrrrrrrrrrriiiiiiiiiiiin nnnnnnnnnnssssssssss* and we were desperately trying to change clothes and wipe off make-up and clear up all our stuff at once, but you know how if you're trying to hurry up somehow things weirdly take twice as long? Plus, I hadn't realized how many bits and bobs we'd got spread everywhere and how eveningy and massively obvious our make-up was, so we *really* had to take it off 'cos no way would we get away with coming out in broad daylight still wearing it.

But then things went from bad to ~~worse~~ ~~disastrous~~ catastrophical. ←

If I could think of a worse word than this to use I would, but this is the worst I can think of in my state of upsetness. I just want to prepare you 'cos what happened next was v.v.v. bad.

Mr. Cain is the Fire Safety Officer (as well as the School Uniform Police) and what happened was he came bursting into the toilets shouting, "Male teacher entering!" and marched round the corner to the second block of loos and saw us all **NOT** exactly in our uniforms and **NOT** in no make-up and with all our *Style School* stuff surrounding us.

We all just froze, staring at him in **TOTAL TERROR**.

"Outside," he shouted. "NOW!" and we got sent out, just like we were, with cleanser all over our faces and only half wearing our uniforms with home clothes on the other parts (I myself had my school skirt on all twistedly over my sequin jeans 'cos I didn't have time to take them off, and my school shirt was done up wrong with no tie).

When we got outside the whole entire school was lined up in their classes behind their teachers, who were doing the registers (there wasn't any actual fire though). So suddenly it was like a million eyes were on us as everyone turned and saw the utter mess we looked like.

Before today, I would have thought I'd die of *mortification* at just *that*, but what happened then was way worse and yet I am still here, alive. How is that possibly possible??

What happened then was that Mr. Cain yelled at us. I mean really YELLED. Not in that "I am pretending to be cross to get you all to shut up and listen" way that teachers do, or like when they act as if they don't find botty burps amusing so that you stop giggling, but really **YELLED** as though he meant it with every stricty bone in his body.

"How **DARE** you not come out of the school when the fire bell goes!" he **YELLED**. "This is an **EXTREMELY** serious matter. You were clearly doing something you shouldn't have been and this **DANGEROUS** situation was the result. Well, what was it?"

Sunny mumblingly went, "*Style School*, sir."

Mr. Cain looked really smug. (I bet he arranged the fire drill on purpose, to find out what we were up to.) I don't blame Sunny for telling, though. One of us would have had to, in the end.

"And who is the ringleader of this, this, *Style School*?" he spat, as if the words *Style School* tasted like slug soup.

That was when my knees almost gave way and I was hanging on to Jemma to stop myself from falling over. I knew I had to own up, or the girls would get in even more trouble. "Me, sir," I said

123

quietly. Then I had this idea that if I tried to explain it a bit he might realize that it wasn't that bad really, so I went, "Sir, it's only a club for trying out new fashions and make-up. It's just a bit of harmless fun."

But it didn't work 'cos Mr. Cain bellowed, "Fun is never harmless! And during school hours too! You should not have been inside over the lunch break and you certainly should not have been wasting your time on something as FRIVOLOUS and RIDICULOUS as fashion!"

Well, I was really scared by then, but no way could I let him get away with saying such terrible things, so I took a deep breath and tried to control my shaking knees and went, "It's not frivolous and ridiculous, though, sir. Fashion is creative and inspiring and for me it's also career development 'cos I'm going to be a fashion designer and—"

His single eyebrow shot right up then and he yelled, "Enough of this RUBBISH!" And I went into completely stunned silence, like, *instantly*.

124

I can't believe he said those things about fashion! Or that I actually wrote them in here, my lovely journal. But it does feel better to get it out of my head and down on paper. I can always rip that page out later, I suppose. Anyway, you can imagine how I felt after he basically said that my one big ambition is rubbish. Actually words can't describe it, apart from maybe the word DEMOLISHED, 'cos it was like I was a house and Mr. Cain was a huge wrecking ball taking a big swing at me and just completely flattening me into the ground. You probably won't be surprised to hear that I started crying.

My head went kind of woozy then and I thought Mr. Cain would start shouting again, but Mr. Wright had come striding over and instead Mr. Cain just gave me an evil piercing stare and stalked off. Mr. Wright quietly sent us back into the loos to get properly changed and clear our stuff up, and then after that we were supposed to go to the secretaries' office and wait for him.

We hardly even looked at each other in the loos and we were in total silence – I think it was 'cos of the shock. We just got ready and packed our things away super fast and hurried to the office. When we got there, Mr. Wright was already waiting for us, with Mr. Cain. I didn't feel so scared of him because of Mr. Wright being there, but I still couldn't look at him at all, and my stomach was flipping over and over as I remembered him shouting at me and embarrassing me in front of the whole school.

Mr. Cain was about to speak but Mr. Wright waved his hand, stopping him, and said to us, "You are all aware that you've broken the school rules by staying indoors at lunchtime when you should have been outside in the playground?"

"Yes, sir," we mumbled, looking at the floor.

"And you know that if we'd found out about

this *style school* we would have banned it during school hours?"

"Yes, sir," we all went, in a chorus of miserability.

"And also that Fire Safety is an extremely serious issue and had there been a real fire you would have been putting your lives at risk and possibly those of others by not exiting the building immediately?"

"Yes, sir," we said again, and I was thinking how I had never heard Mr. Wright be this serious EVER and that the Fire Safety rules must be more important than I realized.

He did a long sigh as if he was completely despairing of us, which was just awful when he is so cool and nice and he organized the battle of the bands and the WORD magazine and all that to make school more fun. "Right, well, you will stay behind tomorrow and copy out the Fire Safety rules 20 times," he said. "Please come back here at 3.30 today to collect letters informing your parents of your detention." He stopped to do another big sigh, then went, "Off you go."

We didn't say anything back, instead we were just shuffling off down the corridor. The Year 7 girls actually have Mr. Wright next for English, so they had to go straight there, but I quickly came into the loos for a bit of tissue to blow my nose and here I still am. I really have to stop crying in a minute, 'cos I am *soooooo* late for science, but I just can't seem to.

Oh, help, someone has just come in.

It's Jules and Tilda, calling for me.

Jules has probably come to say, *serves you right, so there!*

At home at last,
curled up on my bed.

Guess what? At least there is a silver lining to the cloud of awfulness that has been hanging over my day.

Jules and Tilda were sent by Mrs. Stepton to find me (which is why they came into the loos) and instead of saying, *serves you right, so there!* Jules put her arm round me and said, "**HOW DARE** Mr. Cain say that fashion is frivolous and ridiculous and rubbish! Just 'cos *he* thinks that doesn't mean anyone else does! And when you are the best fashion designer in the world, he'll have to eat his Sergeant Major boots, so there!"

"The worst thing is that it happened in front of everyone," I said snifflingly.

"No, that was a *good* thing," Tilda insisted. "They all heard how out of line he was. I'm sure that's why Mr. Wright came and took over. You

129

poor thing, Lucy, it must have been awful. Shouting at kids till they cry is *not* part of Teacher Training!"

After listening to them I felt angry with Mr. Cain instead of just **DEMOLISHED** by him and suddenly I became full of furious power and I was like, "You're right! Fashion is **NOT** rubbish and I will be a designer if I want! It's not my fault that he is unfulfilled 'cos his secret ambition is to be a Sergeant Major but instead he ended up as a teacher for some weird reason! That doesn't mean he can demolish my ambitions and no way will he succeed!"

"Go, Lucy! Go, Lucy!" sang Jules, and Tilda gave me an extra-supportive squeeze. They both knew that I only partly felt like that and partly still felt just mega-upset, but it was better than feeling *completely* upset.

"Erm, Jules, I can't help noticing that you are apparently now talking to me," I said.

"And I also can't help noticing that you are talking to me back," said Jules.

Tilda quickly said, "This shows that when something really bad happens we all come through for each other despite our silly fallings-out, doesn't it?" Then she did a *Meaningful Stare* at me, then at Jules.

I thought Jules might say, "No," then and get in a mood with me again, but luckily she said, "Yes," and also, "Sorry for getting jealous of the Year 7s and thinking they were taking you away, Lu. I know now that they aren't but that they just want to learn about fashion."

"That's okay," I said, "and I'm sorry for going on about them and *Style School* so much. And for forgetting about your Drama Showcase rehearsal...and Tilda's piano exam, of course. I *did* honestly forget, but Mum made me realize that I was wrong for not making more effort to remember."

"That's okay," said Jules, "and sorry for saying you lied. I was just angry. I believe you didn't now."

"That's all right then," I said. Then I took a

deep breath and gabbled, "Look, supporting you two is really important to me and I'll prove that in future if you give me another chance."

I looked hopefully at Tilda. "Course we will, silly!" she said and gave me a big hug.

"*Definitelissimo*," said Jules, joining in.

So now we are friends again and I did know the right thing to do, in the end, just like Mum said. Which turned out to mean being a real *stand-up Babe* and saying sorry and not worrying about how much % of the fault was whose. Even in the middle of all the mess that had become my life, I felt a tiny bit proud of myself.

"And don't worry about Mr. Cain," said Jules then. "We'll show him that fashion is not rubbish but really important. I just don't know how yet."

Me and Jules wanted to stay there in the loos and plot our revenge on Mr. Cain, but sensible Tilda said we had to go straight back to science *right now* or there would be another search party out looking for *us*.

When we got there, by a miracle Mrs. Stepton didn't tell me off for not coming on time and having to be searched for. She just gave me a smile and a rumpled-up tissue from the giant pocket of her baggy cardigan, then carried on with the lesson, going, "Right, now we're going to do an experiment in pairs," and she did this quick thing of counting heads and went, "Oh, we have an odd number today."

Jules linked arms with us and called out, "It's okay, Miss, we'll go as a three because we actually *are* a three in real life!"

Mrs. Stepton said, "Jolly good," and I was thinking, yes it *is* jolly good that we managed to get over the obstacles of life and be friends again and we must have a really strong friendship to be able to do that.

So we were doing the experiment, which was something about acids and alkalines that I did not entirely get, and while we were doing it I got Jules to tell me all about the Drama Showcase, and she

133

said how her fake wart fell off into the cauldron and they all burst out laughing, but apart from that it went fabbly. It was so nice being friends again and just chatting about our normal things in our normal way.

After a while, Mrs. Stepton came and leaned over me and went, "Are you okay now, Lucy, after what happened at lunch?"

"Fine, thanks, Miss," I said quietly, concentrating on the, well, I can't remember now, but the thing I was doing with the litmus paper.

"You know you can achieve anything you set your mind to, don't you?" she said then. "The world is your oyster, or should I say, your *catwalk*."

"Thanks, Miss," I went, and that's when I had the **REVELATION** that Jules is 100% right and that other people don't in fact think what I want to do is stupid, even if Mr. Cain does.

Then Mrs. Stepton said to all three of us, "Any ideas for your stall yet, girls?" and we had to admit that no *Creative Inspirations* were hovering on the horizon at the moment (now we are **BFF** again I am back doing the Charity Fayre – *yay!!!*).

"You'd better come up with something quick smart!" she said, frowning. "Think of all those kids less fortunate than you who really need the money we raise."

I said, "We'll try massively hard to think of something today, Miss, promise."

Then Mrs. Stepton watched while we carried on with our experiment and when we got a bit muddled up she pointed at our bottles of, erm, thingamiwatsit and said, "What you need to do is put the *two together* to make a *solution*."

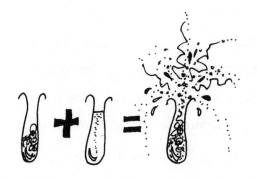

And suddenly I *did* get struck with a *Creative Inspiration*, which was that Mrs. Stepton was not just talking about the science but about how we could put the *two* things of proving Mr. Cain wrong and thinking of something for the Charity Fayre stall *together* to make a *solution* to both problems. Cool, huh? Maybe science is quite useful after all – so long as you think Beyond The Obvious to the secret psychic meanings underneath.

I got madly excited about my idea then and I couldn't even wait till the bell to share it with Jules and Tilda. The problem was that we were going into the bit of the lesson where you quietly write up what you've done, so I couldn't just tell them straight out (also, someone might have been earwigging on us and it has to be top secretly secret). So instead I wrote my idea down in the back of my science book and showed it to J and T, who thought it was *fabulicious!*

So when the lesson ended we hung back till

everyone had left and then we told Mrs. Stepton all about our plan. She also thought it was *fabulicious*, although she didn't say that word obviously, because it is a secret thing between me and Jules and Tilda, the three **BFF**. (It is *soooooo* cool that we have made up!)

Tilda looked a bit worried then and said, "I do think Lucy's idea is really good, but you don't think that *someone* might complain about it, do you, Miss?"

Mrs. Stepton smiled. "No one can complain about you girls raising money for charity," she said and gave me a wink. "But best keep it under your hats till Friday anyway."

I said, "Not that we *have* hats to keep it under, but I get what you mean that it should be most toppily top secret and I agree."

So that was all sorted and now we just have loads to do to prepare for it – cool or what?!

After school when I went to get my detention letter I also passed round my science book so the

Style School girls could read about the Charity Fayre plan, and I whispered, "If you're in, waggle your little finger." And they all did! That is so cool 'cos it will work much better with all of us and we should raise loads more money for charity and also Jules won't mind 'cos of her not being jealous any more. I also whispered to them to wear immaculate uniform till Friday, so Mr. Cain thinks he's completely reformed us into not liking fashion at all. Plus, I said we must be on our best behaviour 'cos after the *Style School* crisis, he will be watching us with the eyes in the back of his head peeled like a hawk, so we can't risk getting in any trouble with him before the Charity Fayre or we might get banned from taking part and we need all of us there to make it the most successful stall that it can possibly be.

I know you are *dying of desperation* to know what we are planning but I don't dare write anything specified down about it in this journal just in case it falls into the wrong hands (and I think you know whose hands are the wrong hands!). Also, I couldn't stick the plan in here 'cos I have ripped it out of the back of my science book and cut it up into tiny little pieces with Mum's nail scissors so no one with the wrong hands can possibly get their wrong hands on it. So v. v. sorry you can't find out all the details yet, but I'm sure you understand I have to keep it top secret.

Oh, GULP, Mum has just called up that it's dinner. Now I have to give her my detention letter and explain all about what happened today, which I have mainly been avoiding since I got home.

Unluckily for me, the detention letter will bring up the whole thing about how *Style School* was maybe not exactly an Official Lunchtime Activity as such.

Oh well, better go and face the music, or the *shouting*, more likely.

We just had tea

and I had a quite bad telling-off, but not too bad – *phew!*.

$\mathcal{I}$ just had to tell Mum all of what happened today and try to get her on my side before showing her the detention letter (groan!). While I was telling her, I had a big lump in my throat and it was really hard to make my fish fingers go down. At first when I was explaining it, Mum was saying things like, "Well, honestly, Lucy!" and "For goodness' sake!" and "WHEN A FIRE BELL GOES YOU GET OUT OF THE BUILDING IMMEDIATELY, DO YOU UNDERSTAND??!!"

To subtly bring in about the detention, I said, "Don't worry, Mum, I will properly understand the vital importance of Fire Safety after tomorrow, 'cos Mr. Wright has thoughtfully allowed us to stay for an hour after school and copy out the Fire

Safety rules 20 times as a learning tool so we know them off by heart."

Mum blinked at me, going, "Lucy Jessica Hartley, is that your way of trying to tell me you've got a detention?"

Alex quickly finished eating and took his chance to leave the table – lucky thing, I wish I could've done!

"Erm, kind of," I went quietly, then I had a big coughy-chokey fit – honestly, why do they make the covering on fish fingers so impossibly hard and scratchy?

Mum banged me on the back and then said, "I can understand why – Fire Safety is a serious issue. But surely the teacher supervising your club should have led you all out? It hardly seems fair that their incompetence be taken out on you—"

I just had to interrupt Mum then 'cos it was *facing the music* time. "Well, there wasn't a teacher supervising as *such*," I muttered, "because *style school* wasn't exactly an official school club, but I'm sure it soon would have become—"

Mum interrupted *me* then. "How could you, Lucy?" she shouted. "You led me to believe it was fine with the teachers—"

"But I didn't *say* it was in those actual words," I cried, interrupting her back, "and anyway, it's unfair that just 'cos we have one stricty teacher we can't express our creativity and have fun and—"

Mum cut me off with her mega-serious stare. "Don't try and justify this," she said. "You knew it wasn't really allowed."

"Well, I sort of thought maybe it wasn't but I really, really wanted to do it and—"

"And so you just convinced yourself it was okay, didn't you?" Mum snapped.

I nodded, feeling full of miserability. "Mum, I am so sorry," I said, with all my deepest sincereness. "I promise you nothing like this will ever happen again."

Mum must have realized from the look on my face that I completely and utterly meant it with every single bit of bone and blood and goop inside my body, 'cos she put out her hand and said, "Shake on it?" And so I did, straight away, 'cos I have never felt more serious about keeping a promise in my whole life. "If you really want something that badly, Lucy, you have to be prepared to stand up and fight for it, not sneak in by the back door..." she began, then stopped herself and did a big sigh. "Okay, look, enough," she said instead. "Let's draw a line under it and move on."

I did a line in the air with my finger to show I totally agreed with her. Then I was moving on by clearing away the plates when she went, "Oh, goodness, Lucy, I've just had a thought. It says in *How To Divorce Without Messing Up Your Kids* that children can act out their negative emotions after a parental split by getting into trouble at school. I'd been secretly worrying about that, and now you've got a detention. Maybe the situation with me and your dad is sending you off the rails!"

I knew I could try and get sympathy, pretending I was still massively upset about Dad **CRUELLY ABANDONING** us, but this was the first chance for me to put my proper *Stand-up Babe* honesty to the test and so I decided to tell the 100% truth. "Mum, to be honest it was really truly just about *Style School*," I said, putting my arm round her, 'cos she looked really worried. "It was a crime of fashion."

That made her laugh, but then she quickly pulled on her *I don't find this amusing at all, Lucy Jessica Hartley* face to show me it was still a *Serious Matter*.

But she didn't have to do that. I *know* it is. And I really, really want to be a proper *Stand-up Babe* instead of just thinking I'm one when I'm not.

Then because we were okay again, I ended up

telling her about Mr. Cain shouting at me about how **FRIVOLOUS** and **RIDICULOUS** fashion is, and saying I was talking **RUBBISH** when I just quietly mentioned about wanting to be a designer. Mum listened with this look of tight-lippedness on her face and then she gave me a big hug and said, . "How do you feel about it now?"

"Okay-ish," I said. "Jules and Tilda helped me realize he wasn't saying what everyone else really thinks."

"Too right!" Mum cried. "It sounds to me like he was that close," and she did a little pinch of air with her fingers, "to being completely out of order. Lucy, if anything like that happens again, you must tell me straight away and I'll be down that school faster than, erm..."

"A rocket-powered skier?" I suggested.

"Precisely," said Mum. "And, see, I told you it would blow over with Jules and Tilda, didn't I?"

"Yep, you were right. You're so full of wisdom, lovely mummy. And seeing as Mr. Cain was so

145

mean and unfair, maybe you could write a note to get me out of—" I began hopefully.

Mum laughed then, going, "Oh, no way! You did the crime, so you have to do the time. Pass me that letter."

So she signed the detention letter and tomorrow I will have to do the *time* for my *crime* like she says, but at least she didn't go all screamy-shouty or even worse, just her

Me doing the time for my crime

completely cold and silent kind of *furiosity*, and she didn't think what Mr. Cain said was true either.

<u>Tuesday,</u>
waiting for Mum to
pick me up after the
detention.

Can't write much. Hand aches. I did my *time*
without looking at Mr. Cain even once. My
burning rage about him dissing my dreams made
me stab the pen in the paper quite hard so it
ripped a bit and got covered in inky blobs, but that
is the best he is getting, so there! Have to rest
hand now.

<u>5.22 o'clock,</u>
at home.
Hand recovering well.

After detention I gave the *style school* girls the
top-secret instruction of meeting in the science
room at lunchtime tomorrow to make stuff to sell

on our Charity Fayre stall, which I think is officially called your *wares*. I can tell you one thing that is not too top secretly secret, which is that we are going to do bag charms, which are *soooooo* trendy at the mo and plus, it tells you how to make them in **Hey Girls!** so I have got plenty of ideas, plus loads of scraps of material and beads and buttons and all that from my sewing box.

Sorry I still can't tell you about the most top secret secret thing we are doing, but I just don't dare write it down in case by some disaster Mr. Cain finds it. I know you can write stuff down and then quickly eat the paper if a teacher tells you to hand it over, which they do on those American high school comedy shows, but I don't know if it works in real life or if you would in fact just choke and die, so best not to risk it!

Wednesday,

after the bag charm-
making session.

Well, I can report that our bag charms look totally fab! I brought in all the stuff, like:

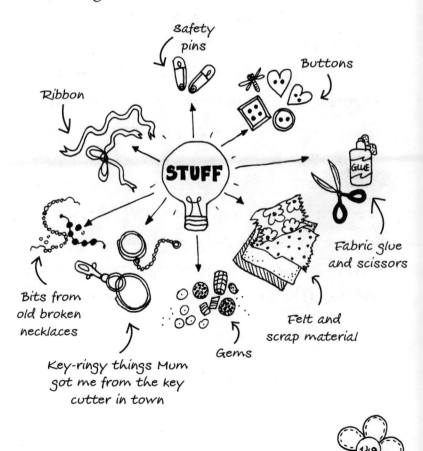

Safety pins

Buttons

Ribbon

Fabric glue and scissors

Bits from old broken necklaces

STUFF

Felt and scrap material

Gems

Key-ringy things Mum got me from the key cutter in town

It was *soooooo* cool 'cos Mrs. Stepton let us use the science room at lunchtime while she was in and out setting up for the next lesson. We all sat along one side of a workbench and made different charms and then we passed the plain key rings along and everyone added one thing to each one.

It was even cooler that Jules and Tilda and the *Style School* girls were all sitting happily next to each other without Jules getting jealous, and even, even cooler that we were all singing while we worked, doing the harmonies like in proper girl bands.

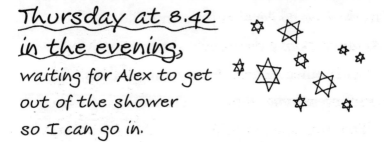

Thursday at 8.42 in the evening,

waiting for Alex to get out of the shower so I can go in.

I am just quickly scribbling this to say that we worked all this lunchtime too, and including yesterday's we have made 62 bag charms altogether! Here are some of the designs:

So I'm really excited 'cos now we've got some brilliant *wares* for our stall.

Thank goodness the last day of wearing my uniform correctly is finally over and tomorrow it is the Charity Fayre and also *Wear What You Want* day. I am sick of people sniffing me and going, "Poo, you smell of fish! Oh, it must be that kipper you're wearing!" I mean, ha ha, **NOT**!

Still, it will be worth it when we reveal our secret plan tomorrow.

Oh, Alex is out of the bathroom now and I've got to go in the shower and get in my nightie. Then I will carry on with my secret planning for tomorrow, when I'll get my fab revenge on Mr. Cain.

HA-HA-HAAAAAA!!!

Evil-genius laugh!

Friday before school!

I have woken up really
early with the excitement,
as in at 6.27 a.m.!!

At last, it is time to tell you my secret plan to get revenge on Mr. Cain!

The secret plan is that:

⟡ ✿
✿   *It is non-uniform day, but we are*   ✿
✿   *in actual fact going in school uniform!*   ✿
✿ ✿

What??? you are most probably thinking. *Lucy Jessica Hartley, have you gone completely INSANE???*

No, is the answer to that, but *Mr. Cain* will when he sees what we have done to our uniforms, and then that will be my revenge!

HA-HA-HAAAAAA! ←

Evil-genius laugh again!

That is because it **IS** school uniform, but not as we know it. For example, I have just put mine on, and it looks like:

Loads of sparkly hairslides →

Superlonglash Mascara ←

← Little plaits

Shimmery silver Moondust lipgloss ←

Cool badges →

Unkipper-ish tie ←

Studded belt →

Loads of bangles ←

Skirt rolled up →

Non-regulation purple and pink flowery tights ↙

My new boots ↘

I got the idea from ages ago when I was thinking about pushing the boundaries of School

Uniform one bit at a time – but then I realized that if it was officially a Non-Uniform Day then I could push every single boundary all at once! And Mr. Cain wouldn't be able to do anything about it!! And *that* would be the ultimate revenge!!!

> **HA-HA-HAAAAAA!!!**

Sorry I keep writing this, but it is sooooooo fun to do out loud at the same time!

The Charity Fayre starts at morning break for two hours, and then we have a late lunch and a whole school assembly last thing, and then it is home time, so only one double lesson all day and that's only English! **Yay!**

I have got my fingers crossed in my head that it all goes well. Other people have got brilliant stall ideas so we probably won't win the actual prize. But I really hope we'll raise loads for the *Giving Inner City Kids Some Fields* charity, and I know our stall will still be massively, mega-ly fun and also the world's greatest revenge on a teacher!

And you will find out what exactly we are doing on the stall *v. v. soon* – promise!

Wish us luck!

At school,

very quickly writing
this before the Charity
Fayre starts.

I am just quickly writing this in the school
secretaries' office. No, I'm not in trouble again –
phew! – but I am in fact waiting while Mrs.
Smith finds me some more Blu-tack for sticking
stuff up on our stall. Me, Jules and Tilda had
English first thing and the look on Mr. Wright's
face when he saw our outfits was *soooooo* funny –
hee hee!

He went, "Hmm, very creative and original,
girls. This will totally serve Mr. Cain right!"

Well, of course he didn't say that last bit in
actual *words*, but I could almost hear him
thinking it (my powers of psychicness are getting
stronger all the time). Jemma just told me they
had Mrs. Stepton first thing, so Mr. Cain has not

yet seen any of us – *double hee hee!*

We got off lessons 10 minutes early to set up our stalls before break, and I was wowed by the fabness of the *Style School* girls' transformed uniforms and I have been saying things like, "Carla, it's so great the way you've tied that shirt up to show your belly button," and, "Those red hair mascara streaks look amazing, Sunny," and, "Excellent skirt length, Jemma, it looks like a belt," etc. etc. It is really satisfying to think that everything I have taught them has really sunk in and they have done such fab make-up and accessorizing and customizing, all on their own.

Plus, Jules has made us all these cool badges that say:

When she rang me up last night she wanted to put "We won't be stopped from following our passion and expressing ourselves in a creative media we love", but I had to suggest cutting it down a bit, so people could get the point quickly and didn't have to stand there staring at the badges for ages.

Lizzie and Carla created a cool *style school* banner for the stall, and Jemma made a fab *totalometer* in the shape of a lipstick by sticking loads of bits of paper end to end to end. The girls loved the funky sign I drew last night (Alex helped 'cos there was a lot of felt-tipping to do). It's like this:

HAIRSTYLING = £1

NAIL POLISH = £1
AND NAIL TATTOOS!

MAKE-UP = £1

FULL MAKEOVER = £2·50
(INCLUDING EVERYTHING !!!)

PLUS BUY OUR
FAB BAG CHARMS = £2 each
FOR ONLY

So, *da daaaaaa*!!!!!

I can now officially reveal that our other top secretly secret plan is to give *Style School*-type makeovers to everyone, and as Mrs. Stepton says, 'cos it's for charity Mr. Cain can't complain (hopefully!). Also it will show him that fashion is not rubbish but vital, 'cos of it raising loads of dosh for a good cause!

Oh cool, the Blu-tack has arrived – gotta go!

Well, the Charity Fayre

has now happened
and it was fabulissimo!!!

I have just been to the Cool Cats café and had
a yummy burger and milkshake with all the *style
school* girls and Jules and Tilda, for reasons that
I will reveal to you later.

First I will write about the Charity Fayre,
which went fabbly. You might even want to get
a drink or a snack or whatever, and settle down
somewhere cosy to read this 'cos there is *loads*
to tell you. I just want to say everything in a big
rush, but I will make myself write it down one
thing at a time and in scientifically logical order.
(Mrs. Stepton would be so proud of me, well she
is anyway after today!)

So, let me start from where I left off, which
was when I got given the Blu-tack.

When I got given the Blu-tack I went back

outside and the girls were all laying out the stuff for the makeovers. It was so cool 'cos we put chairs around the stall and set up our mirrors brought from home. We'd also brought in all the hair and make-up and nail bits we had and set it up like real professional make-up artists and hairstylists and nail painters. (Mum wouldn't lend me her MAC stuff for it, which was lucky in the end 'cos we had so many customers things got kind of run down and messed up.) I even took the stuff down off my pinboard at home and brought the board in for displaying the bag charms on, and everyone brought in any old or spare hairbands and clips and slides to use for the hairstyling. When we'd finished working our *style school* magic the stall looked completely fab.

Then the bell went for break and everyone came piling out of school and the Charity Fayre officially began.

Jules started yelling, "Roll up! Roll up! Buy your unique bag charms here for only £2! They're handcrafted locally by happy workers!" That was great but I had to stop her when she got a bit overenthusiastic and started picking people out and yelling at them, "Come to our stall – you look like you really need a makeover!"

But Jules didn't have to shout the rolling-up thing for long 'cos we got loads of customers. And this is what we were doing:

1) Jules was shouting the rolling-up thing and selling the bag charms.
2) Jemma and me were doing the full makeovers when people wanted absolutely everything (it was fun both working on one person at the same time!).
3) Sunny was in charge of knock-out nails.

4) Carla was doing magical make-up.

5) Lizzie created fab hairstyles.

6) Tilda was busy working out how much we'd
   made without even using a calculator and
   moving the lipstick totalometer up.

It was so good, 'cos after about half an hour we
got a crowd gathering, all waiting for their turns.
There were even some boys lurking around to see
which girls they might start to fancy after their
transformations!

The bag charms sold really well, and in fact
Jules spotted one of the okay boys from our class
(Jamie Cousins to be precise!) buying them from
the stall for £2 and selling them for £3 so she *Had
a Word* with him. I don't know the exact word
she had with him but it had the right effect 'cos he
"generously" donated all his profits from the bag
charms back to our stall. Then Jules put the price
up to £3 to see what would happen and people still
kept buying them, so we left it like that!

We got so into running our stall that we totally forgot about getting revenge on Mr. Cain, or even wondering where he was. But then suddenly his head was looming above the crowd, and his single eyebrow went shooting up towards the sky as he saw our uniforms.

Well, I can now report that he went completely **INSANE** just as I was hoping. He was stuttering and stammering but no actual words were coming out. And his eyes were staring and boggling at what we were wearing and then suddenly he found some words and went, "What is the meaning of this?!"

I decided to *Take The Bull by The Horns*, as Mum calls it (weird phrase, I wonder if anyone has actually *done* that for real and still stayed alive??) and called out, "But, sir, we're wearing our uniforms even though we can wear whatever we want today. You should be pleased!"

Mr. Cain's eyes popped even more bulgingly out of his head than they had already and he roared, "You know full well you're advertising how to break the uniform code! Half the school will be copying your ideas by Monday!"

I put on my best innocent face and went, "Oh, I'm sure they won't, sir. After all, as you said, fashion is **FRIVOLOUS** and **RIDICULOUS**, so why would anyone want to copy what we're doing?!"

Mr. Cain looked like he was trying to hold down a really huge burp then, and started going the colour of livid, which is not good for anyone's health. He looked so furious I started to panic that the next thing he was going to say would be "Pack up this nonsense and get to the office **NOW**!" but thank goodness Mrs. Stepton came along with her perfect scientific timing and saved us.

She was amazed by how much we'd raised (so were we to be honest!) and congratulated us on our fab stall and brill ideas. "I knew you'd do a great stall, girls," she said loudly (I'm sure it was so Mr. Cain would hear). "You're so full of great ideas and creative talent!"

Mr. Cain obviously *did* hear because he turned on her and went, "But, Mrs. Stepton, surely you can see that this is deliberate disobedience? This silly *style school* business has been banned!"

All us girls held our breaths, and our nail polishes and powder brushes and combs and that were all paused in mid-air, desperately hoping Mrs. Stepton wouldn't back down. Mr. Cain can be scary even if you're a teacher, he is *that* stricty.

Luckily, Mrs. Stepton just smiled and said, "I understood that the objections to *style school* were about not responding to the fire alarm and being inside the school at lunchtime. That is not what's happening here. And look how much they've raised – it's fantastic! Besides, I authorized this stall so if you have any complaints about it we should really talk in private."

Mr. Cain gave her a complete *Look of Poison* and muttered, "We'll discuss this later," before stalking off into the school.

We really had to clamp our lips together so we

didn't giggle and I thought Mrs. Stepton might say something about what had just happened, but of course she is completely professional so she didn't. Even fabber, she went, "You know what, I fancy a full makeover myself. Blue nails I think; let's go for a change." She got her big fat purse out of the giant pocket on the front of her baggy cardigan, and I was thinking how amazing it is that some people can wear Scholl sandals and baggy cardies all their life and still be totally cool!

Later on, we sold completely out of bag charms, so we had a spare person. We all swapped round jobs after that to give everyone a chance to go and see what else was happening. When it was my turn for a break I went over and looked at the Circus Skills stall, which was cool 'cos they were doing "Learn to juggle" (apparently they'd started off doing "Learn to juggle with fire clubs" until Mrs. Stepton made them change to PE beanbags instead). I didn't feel like guessing how many sweets there were in a jar *(yawn!)* on the Year

9 girls' stand, but I did try riding on the Crazy Bike that won't go straight and tips you off, which Harry the mechanical whizz-kid of Year 10 invented.

Then I got to Simon Driscott and the Geeky Minions' stall. In the end their Virtual Reality machine turned out to be not that amazing, due to it being actually really hard to make one — especially in only a week in a school computer lab, as Simon pointed out to me.

"Hmm, so basically it is now not Virtual Reality but simply playing a computer game for five minutes in a black tent," I observed.

SD blushingly admitted that I was right, but I didn't want to be non-supportive so I added, "Well, I think it's really good."

"Thanks, Lucy," he said. "It's just a shame that people are not even playing the computer game but just using the tent to kiss in!" He shuddered, as if that was the most disgusting thing he'd ever heard. Then he barred the way to Augusta Rinaldi and Bill Cripps, who are actually going out since Tilda's second party, and went, "One at a time only!" all harrassedly. He looked even more stressed when they ignored him and went in together anyway.

"Oh, I'd just let them in," I said, shrugging. "After all, it's double the money for charity."

"I suppose so," grumbled Simon, "but they are not *properly appreciating* our stall."

That's when I decided to cheer him up by *properly appreciating* it my actual self, so I went, "I will have a go, but you'll have to come in with me."

Simon Driscott blushed bright red again and found some important staring at the floor to do. I was wondering why till I suddenly realized he thought I wanted to go in there with him for *kissing purposes!*

"No, you divvock!" I cried. "Why would I want to do *that* when we are just sort of friends with no fancying going on whatsoever? It's just that to *properly appreciate* your work I need you to show

171

me how to operate the *technologicality*."

"You mean technology," he said correctingly, in that annoying way he does.

"Yeah, like, whatever," I went.

"Yeah, like, whatever," he said back, and I realized that he was doing an impression of me!

"Ha ha, NOT!" I went, pretending to think he is the Prince of Pillockdom (but in fact I still think that he is quite funny and okay).

So I had a go in the black tent thing and it was quite cool, if you like sitting in the dark bashing aliens over the head with a laser rod.

It was so funny then, 'cos I got back to our stall and this photo-journalist from the local paper had come to report on the Charity Fayre and was about to take pictures of us. "Quick, Lucy!" called Jemma. "You've got to be in the middle 'cos you're the one who thought of all this!"

So I squeezed in and we had our pix taken, which was really cool, especially 'cos Mr. Cain tried to get his head between us and the camera but the photographer just went, "Could you move out of the way, please, sir?" and he had to do what he was told, hee hee!

Then the bell went for late lunch and the Charity Fayre started winding down as people headed inside. Our *style school* stall final total of money raised was an amazing

It was off the scale and we actually had to draw more lines on the lipstick totalometer to fit it on!

We packed up our stall and put our stuff away in the secretaries' office, and then we went in for lunch. It was really cool 'cos we all sat on a table together and people kept coming up and saying, "Cool uniforms!" and they were obviously *Getting Ideas* for what to do with theirs!

HA-HA-HAAAAAA!!!

173

Then the most fabulous of fabulicious things happened 'cos it was Friday afternoon assembly and Mr. Phillips announced the total amount of money raised, which was a most staggering £1,649.60! Then he was going to give out the prize for the most money raised on one stall. Me and Jules and Tilda all held hands like on Pop Idol while waiting to find out who it was, and I could see the other *style school* girls doing the same thing a couple of rows in front of us.

And guess what? You might not believe it (I couldn't hardly!) but **WE WON**!!!

The best thing was that we all got to go onstage in front of the whole entire school, including even the sixth form, and Mr. Phillips said how well we'd done and told us to give everyone a twirl of our outfits, which he thought were *jolly good fun*.

"And may I ask who thought up this wonderful idea?" he said.

I wasn't going to say it was me, 'cos of not

sounding like a big-head, but all the other girls said it was so he found out anyway. "Good work, young lady," he said, "you and your team have done extremely well. I understand you want to be a fashion designer when you grow up, and with the ideas and hard work you've put into this, I'm sure you'll achieve your ambition!"

So I was absolutely exploding with pride when he took an envelope out of his pocket and gave it to me, and shook hands with us all while everyone clapped and cheered – except Mr. Cain of course, who pretended to have some urgent tying his shoelace to do. That's when I realized that it doesn't matter if he thinks fashion is rubbish – there will always be people who don't, and they're the ones who really count!

When the clapping had died down, Mr. Phillips said, "And I believe you young ladies even did a makeover on Mrs. Stepton!"

So Mrs. Stepton stood up and did a turn and a model-y pose for the whole school too, and everyone clapped and cheered again, and even when Mr. Cain raised his long bushy eyebrow to restore order no one took any notice 'cos Mr. Phillips was clapping and cheering too, and he is the *actual headmaster*. Days like this are so fun 'cos even the teachers act like normal people! Plus, it was almost like the imagining I had when I first thought of *style school*, about being cheered onstage for my creative uniform campaign!!

I was just absolutely glowing with joy then, and I opened the envelope and read out the prize, which was free burgers and milkshakes at the Cool Cats café (I knew deep down it wouldn't be tickets to New York!). Me and my **BFF** and the *style school* girls all did a squealy jumping-up-and-down huggy thing and then I remembered everyone was watching and it was still school, so I just said a polite thank you to Mr. Phillips and he said, "No, thank *you*," and then we all walked off the stagey bit and everyone clapped again and I really hope I will remember that three minutes for the rest of my life, because I felt like I was on about Cloud 10, which means even happier than Cloud 9.

After assembly it was the end of school, so we all gave our parents a ring and made sure everyone could go to Cool Cats straight away (we wouldn't have gone if even one person couldn't, 'cos of being a team). It was great 'cos when we got into town we all linked arms going up the pedestrian bit to the café, and I didn't mind that me and Jules weren't next to each other in physicalness 'cos I felt closer to her than ever in an emotionality way.

Oh, look, I have completely run out of journal. That is *boo* 'cos I wanted to stick the *style school* stall photo in here when it comes out in the paper, but maybe I will put it on the wall instead. Actually, Mum was so completely impressed with us when I told her about today that she might even insist on framing it!

So anyway, I will most definitely buy a new journal and write soon, especially 'cos I want to tell you if anyone copied our *style school* ideas for their actual official school uniform on Monday!!!

But for now, lots and lots and lots of love and goodbyeness from

Lucy Jessica Hartley xxx

Don't go yet!
My cool quiz is on
the next page...

Lucy Jessica Hartley's Style Quiz

What's your perfect signature look?
Are you a **city chic chick**,
Boho Princess or Trendsetting Babe?
Find your signature style with my fab quiz!

1. You imagine your grown-up self:
A) Twirling round in a field of flowers with your arms stretched out in that way people do on shampoo ads.
B) Strutting your stuff in a funky nightspot after work at your exciting, creative job.
C) Sitting in your giant glass office in a New York skyscraper, going, "Buy, buy, buy, sell, sell, sell!" down the phone.

2. To you, getting dressed up means:
A) Teaming that gypsy skirt with cool boots instead of your usual flip-flops – and maybe adding a dash of lipgloss.

B) Shopping! Any excuse to hit the high street and bag a funky new look!

C) A chance to wear your smart new trousers and try out that swooshy black eyeliner you've been saving.

3. Which of these outfits do you like best?

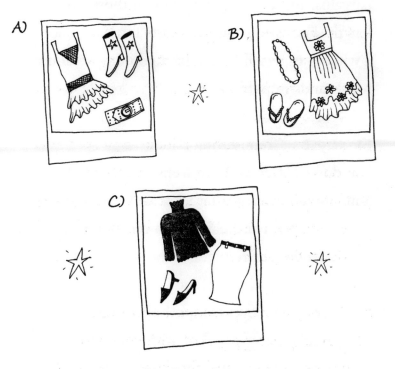

A)

B)

C)

Now, turn over to get your results...

☆ So which one are you? ☆

Mostly As: Boho Princess!
You love the hippy vintage look and this fun individual style really lets you get creative as you search markets and second-hand shops for one-off bargains. But don't forget to ditch those floor-length skirts and jangly bracelets for jeans once in a while – especially when trampolining or doing handstands in public!

Mostly Bs: Trendsetting Babe!
You don't just *follow* the trends, you *set* them! You have an eye for what's hot and what's not, and you create bold and daring combinations that wow your friends. But remember the secret of fashion success – don't try too hard!

Mostly Cs: City Chic Chick!

You're smart and stylish, and you love to coordinate your look from head to toe. You have a great sense of what suits you, but don't forget to experiment too – hold swapsies days with friends to try out new styles without splashing the cash!

Totally Secret Info about Kelly McKain

Lives: In a small flat in Chiswick, West London, with a fridge full of chocolate.

Life's ambition: To be a showgirl in Paris 100 years ago. *(Erm, not really possible that one! – Ed.)* Okay, then, to be a writer – so I am actually doing it – yay! And also, to go on a flying trapeze.

Star sign: Capricorn.

Fave colour: Purple.

Fave animal: Monkey.

Ideal pet: A purple monkey.

Style School blunder: Pretending to have a sore throat so I could wear my funky purple scarf in class – but I kept forgetting to do the croaky voice!

Fave hobbies: Hanging out with my BFF and gorge boyf, watching *Friends*, going to yoga and dance classes, and playing my guitar as badly as Lucy's dad!

Find out more about Kelly at www.kellymckain.co.uk

Have you read all of Lucy's hilarious journals?

Makeover Magic

Lucy Jessica Hartley is a style queen, so when a geeky new girl starts at school, she comes up with a fab Makeover Plan to help her fit in.

0 7460 6689 9   £4.99

Fantasy Fashion

Lucy's fave mag is running a competition to design a fantasy fashion outfit and Lucy is determined to win the fab prize – whatever it takes!

0 7460 6690 2   £4.99

Boy Band Blues

Lucy has been asked to style a boy band for a Battle of the Bands competition and she's mega-excited about it – it's just a shame lead singer Wayne is such a big-head!

0 7460 6691 0   £4.99

Star Struck

Lucy's won a part as a film extra and decides she must get her fab design skills noticed on screen – but will the director appreciate her original efforts?

0 7460 7061 6   £4.99

Picture Perfect

Lucy decides to throw a big surprise party for Tilda's 13th birthday – but will crossed wires wreck her efforts, and their friendship?

0 7460 7062 4   £4.99

All out now!

Coming soon...

Summer Stars

Lucy, Jules and Tilda are off to Newquay on holiday! Even better, their fave mag is holding a beach party in the very same town! Can they win the dance comp and strut their stuff onstage? Or will the Greatest Cringe Of All Time crush their dreams of seaside stardom?

9780746080177   £4.99

Catwalk Crazy

Lucy is putting on a charity fashion show, but someone seems to be sabotaging all her efforts. Can she track down the culprit and win back her audience before it's too late?

9780746080184   £4.99

check out
www.fiction.usborne.com
for more dazzling
and delightfully funny
girl reads

To the totally fab Rebecca Hill,
with love.

First published in the UK in 2006 by Usborne Publishing Ltd., Usborne House, 83-85 Saffron Hill, London EC1N 8RT, England. www.usborne.com

Text copyright © Kelly McKain, 2006.
Illustration copyright © Usborne Publishing Ltd., 2006.

Illustrations by Vici Leyhane.

A CIP catalogue record for this book is available from the British Library.

JFMAMJJASO D/06
ISBN 0 7460 7063 2
Printed in Great Britain.